J

OBI,
Gerbil on the Loose!

OBI,
Gerbil on the LOOSE!

Michael Delaney

Dutton Children's Books

DUTTON CHILDREN'S BOOKS
A division of Penguin Young Readers Group

Published by the Penguin Group
Penguin Group (USA) Inc., 375 Hudson Street, New York, New York 10014, U.S.A.
· Penguin Group (Canada), 10 Eglinton Avenue East, Suite 700, Toronto, Ontario,
Canada M4P 2Y3 (a division of Pearson Penguin Canada Inc.) · Penguin Books Ltd,
80 Strand, London WC2R 0RL, England · Penguin Ireland, 25 St Stephen's Green,
Dublin 2, Ireland (a division of Penguin Books Ltd) · Penguin Group (Australia),
250 Camberwell Road, Camberwell, Victoria 3124, Australia (a division of Pearson
Australia Group Pty Ltd) · Penguin Books India Pvt Ltd, 11 Community Centre,
Panchsheel Park, New Delhi—110 017, India · Penguin Group (NZ), 67 Apollo Drive,
Rosedale, North Shore 0632, New Zealand (a division of Pearson New Zealand Ltd) ·
Penguin Books (South Africa) (Pty) Ltd, 24 Sturdee Avenue, Rosebank, Johannesburg
2196, South Africa · Penguin Books Ltd, Registered Offices:
80 Strand, London WC2R 0RL, England

The publisher does not have any control over and does not assume any responsibility
for author or third-party websites or their content.

CIP DATA IS AVAILABLE

Published in the United States by Dutton Children's Books,
a division of Penguin Young Readers Group
345 Hudson Street, New York, New York 10014
www.penguin.com/youngreaders

Designed by Irene Vandervoort
Printed in USA   First Edition
ISBN: 978-0-525-47890-4

10 9 8 7 6 5 4 3 2 1

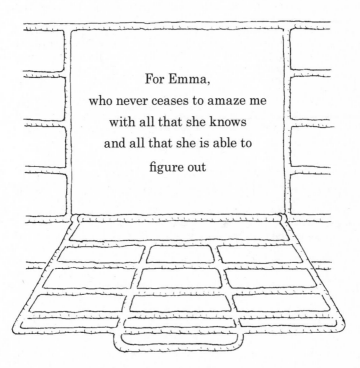

For Emma,
who never ceases to amaze me
with all that she knows
and all that she is able to
figure out

Special thanks to Irwin Glusker.
Once while accepting one of my drawings for
publication, Mr. Glusker, who at the time was the art
director of *Gourmet* magazine, told me he couldn't
promise me *both* fame and fortune, but he could promise
me fame. And for many years, at least among the faithful
readers of *Gourmet* magazine, he did.

contents

Spider?
I'm not a spider!
I'm a hairy, scary tarantula!

OBI,
Gerbil on the Loose!

Looking back on that morning, Obi should have guessed that something strange was up long before she did.

There were, after all, so many clues.

For one thing, Mrs. Armstrong woke Rachel, Obi's adopted mother, super-early that morning, as if Rachel was going to school. But she wasn't going to school. It was the end of June, school was out for the summer, the days were long and sweltering hot, and Rachel should have been allowed to sleep as late as she wanted to—well, within reason, of course.

Another thing that, in retrospect, seemed a bit odd was that Rachel and the rest of her family all seemed to be in unusually bad moods that morning. In fact, there was a tremendous fight at breakfast between Rachel and her older brother, Craig. The argument was over whose music they were going to listen to in the Armstrongs' human mobile—Craig's or Rachel's. Obi could hear their loud, angry voices all the way from upstairs. Mr. Armstrong finally settled the matter. They would take turns on what music got played.

And come to think of it, that, too, was rather peculiar—what was Mr. Armstrong doing home for breakfast? He never was home for breakfast during the week. Indeed, he was always the first one out the door in the morning.

In all likelihood, Obi would have realized something was up with the Armstrongs much sooner than she did if she had been allowed to venture downstairs on her own—the way, for instance, the cats could. But she wasn't allowed. Not that Obi was complaining, mind you. The truth was, Obi had it made. She had a perfectly charming apartment in the upstairs of the Armstrongs' perfectly charming house (which was located in the perfectly charming town of New Canaan, Connecticut). True, it was a small apartment, with just a living room, a kitchen area, and an upstairs bedroom. Still, though a little cramped, the apartment was, by even the most discriminating interior decorator's standards, extremely cozy.

Obi's adopted mother had tastefully and lovingly furnished the place. There was a blue Victorian-style couch; a straight-backed chair of dark mahogany wood that looked as if it might have once belonged to a matching dining-room table set; a rolltop desk that had a lamp with a floral lampshade; a big, fancy armoire; and an ancient refrigerator, circa 1960s, that was a robin's-egg blue in color and had a decal of a yellow happy face slapped across its door. The furniture was forever disappearing under deep mounds of fragrant cedar shavings that covered the floor. But then, that was to be expected. Obi was, after all, a gerbil, and the furniture, which was only a few inches in size, was from Rachel's dollhouse.

To be honest, Obi had no real use for the dollhouse furniture (except to occasionally gnaw on). There were two things, though, that Obi had plenty of use for. One was the squeaky but speedy exercise wheel that was attached to the metal bars of her living room. Obi loved to run on her exercise wheel, and she ran all the time. She spent hours on the screechy contraption, sprinting furiously in place, never going anywhere. While Obi ran, she liked to glance over at the old refrigerator and wonder what could possibly be inside. Since the refrig-

erator door was painted on and did not actually open, she had no way of finding out. In addition to the old refrigerator, her kitchen area contained a hanging water bottle and a small plastic dish that held her gerbil food—grains, sunflower seeds, and the most delicious multicolored yogurt puffballs.

The other love of Obi's life (not counting Rachel, of course) was a clear plastic globe that Rachel called the Gerbil Mobile. Rachel would place Obi inside the globe, close the hatch, and then let Obi wander all about the house. Obi simply had to start running, and off she went. It was just like running on her exercise wheel, only better because she could go wherever she pleased.

Obi's second-floor bedroom was also piled high with cedar shavings. To get up to, and down from, her bedroom, which rose high up into the air like a city skyscraper, Obi had to climb through a rather steep vertical tube that was made of blue transparent plastic. An expert climber, Obi scurried up and down the tube in seconds flat. Obi's bedroom had a domed ceiling that was also made of blue transparent plastic. From her bedroom, Obi had a magnificent, blue-tinted view of her adopted mother's bedroom and all of her belongings: a bunk bed, a desk and chair, a dollhouse, an armchair, a bookcase, a music stand (Rachel played the violin), posters on the walls, and all sorts of toys, books, and games. The floor of Obi's adopted mother's bedroom was not covered with cedar shavings, the way Obi's floors were. Her floor had a yellow carpet.

Looking in the opposite direction, Obi was able to see out her adopted mother's second-floor bedroom window. From this window, Obi could see a big, old, leafy Norway maple that grew out in the front yard.

Obi's apartment sat on Rachel's dresser, along with a lamp, Rachel's hairbrush and a few elastic hair ties, and a framed photo. The photo, a school portrait, was of Obi's adopted mother, smiling. At nine years old, Rachel C. Armstrong was a fourth grader at the local New Canaan elementary school. She had a roundish face, freckles on her nose, the bluest of blue eyes, and shoulder-length brown hair that, more often than not, she wore in a ponytail.

No doubt about it, Obi led a charmed life. The gerbil never had to worry about a thing. Whenever she needed exercise, Obi just hopped on her treadmill and went for a run. Whenever her food dish or water supply ran low, Rachel refilled them. And whenever Obi's apartment needed cleaning out, her adopted mother's mother cleaned it. (Obi preferred to call her home an apartment rather than "a cage." "Apartment" sounded less, well, incarcerating.)

If Obi had any complaints at all, it was with her name. She had a boy's name. To be fair, this was perfectly understandable (and forgivable). Obi had been adopted at birth. She had been only a few days old when Mr. Armstrong and Rachel dropped by the pet store and bought her. At the time, no one had a clue whether the gerbil was a male or a female—not even the woman in the pet store. Rachel, believing Obi to be a male, named the gerbil after her favorite character in *Star Wars*: Obi-Wan Kenobi. In all honesty, Obi would have preferred a girl's name. However, if she was going to have to go through life with a boy's name, she considered herself lucky that it was Obi. There was, after all, a certain pizzazz to being named after Obi-Wan Kenobi.

The gerbil knew all about her namesake. That was because Rachel would often hold Obi in her lap while she watched TV or a rented video or DVD movie. Obi had seen lots of movies—all from the comfort of Rachel's warm, cozy lap. To name just a few, she had seen *The*

Lion King (she certainly was glad there were no hyenas in New Canaan, Connecticut), *Fly Away Home* (an excellent movie in Obi's opinion, but she would have liked the movie even better if gerbils instead of geese had had the starring roles), *The Incredible Journey* (another movie that could have used a gerbil or two), and, of course, the *Star Wars* movies. The little gerbil knew what a fearless, clever, and resourceful Jedi knight Obi-Wan Kenobi was. Obi liked to think that if she ever had to do battle with evil aliens from outer space, she, too, would be just as fearless, clever, and resourceful as the great Obi-Wan Kenobi.

chapter TWO Sweetie Smoochkins

It was the tabby cat, Sweetie Smoochkins, who broke the news to Obi that something was up with the Armstrongs. There were six members of the Armstrong family: Mr. and Mrs. Armstrong; Rachel's older brother, Craig; Rachel; and Betsy and Susie, the identical twins. Each Armstrong had his or her own pet or pets.

Mr. Armstrong had an old yellow Labrador named Mack and a garrulous parrot named Mr. Smithers.

Mrs. Armstrong had three rather evil cats. Each cat had a sugary sweet name: Sweetie Smoochkins, Sugar Smacks, and Honey Buns. Why Mrs. Armstrong had given her cats such sugary sweet names completely baffled Obi, because not one was the least bit kind or sugary sweet to Obi. Obi was also completely baffled as to why Mrs. Armstrong felt she needed three cats when one—or better yet, *none*—would have been more than enough.

Craig, too, had pets—at least that was what Obi had heard. She didn't know for sure, though. That was because Craig's pets lived inside Craig's bedroom, and Craig's bedroom door was always closed. Rachel never ventured into his bedroom, which meant, of course, Obi never did, either. And who could blame Rachel? The outside of Craig's bedroom door was plastered with signs that silently screamed the most hostile warnings: DANGER! HIGH VOLTAGE! STOP! KEEP OUT! BEWARE! NO TRESPASSING! There was even a small black flag with a pirate's skull and crossbones pinned near the doorknob! One look at Craig's bedroom door would scare off even the boldest intruder—and little sister.

The identical twins, Betsy and Susie, each had a goldfish for a pet. The two goldfish—whose names, rather confusingly, were also Betsy and Susie—were just as hard to tell apart as the human Betsy and Susie. The goldfish lived downstairs in the TV room—as did Mack and Mr. Smithers. The fish lived in an aquarium that had a nifty underwater castle.

Not surprisingly, considering she was a cat and Obi was a gerbil, Sweetie Smoochkins did not come right out and tell Obi what she knew. Although that would have been the friendly thing to do, she didn't. What she did do was this: while the Armstrongs were all downstairs in the kitchen eating breakfast, Sweetie Smoochkins, looking her usual bored self, wandered into Rachel's bedroom.

"Hawo, Sweetie Smoochkins!" said Obi with a big, cheerful smile, as if she was delighted to see the cat. She wasn't. The truth was, Obi dreaded whenever one of the cats paid her a visit. Like many small creatures, Obi had an enormous fear of cats. Consequently, she went out of her way to be as nice as possible whenever one stopped by. "So how are you today?" she asked.

Sweetie Smoochkins mumbled something under her breath. Whatever it was, it sounded terribly rude. The cat walked to the foot of the dresser and, without even pausing (let alone asking if Obi was busy or if it was okay to drop by for a visit), she leaped up on top of the dresser. Sweetie Smoochkins gazed hard at Obi inside her apartment. Her tail began to swirl and swish in that awful hypnotic sort of way.

"So what's new?" Obi asked in a polite but nervous voice.

"Haven't you heard?" said Sweetie Smoochkins. She

wiggled her left front paw between two bars of Obi's living room and tried to swat poor Obi.

"Heard what?" asked Obi. Keeping her distance from the cat's groping paw, Obi acted as if this was a perfectly normal way for a guest to behave.

"The news!"

"What news?" asked Obi.

"The big news, Fuzzball!" replied Sweetie Smooch-kins.

"What big news?"

Sweetie Smoochkins gave Obi a shocked look as if she could not believe Obi hadn't heard. "You mean, Rachel hasn't told you?"

"Told me what?"

"The big news!"

"No, I haven't heard anything. What's the big news?"

"Well, it's like this," said the cat. She leaned close to the bars and lowered her voice like she was about to reveal a huge secret. But then she shook her head and said, "You know, maybe I better not say anything."

"Why not?"

"Well, Rachel hasn't said anything to you. Maybe she doesn't want you to know."

"Sure she does!" cried Obi. "I'm her pet!"

"True, true," said Sweetie Smoochkins, nodding.

"She just hasn't had a chance to tell me, that's all," explained Obi. The little gerbil had no idea if this was indeed true, but she hoped it was.

"Well, okay," said Sweetie Smoochkins. "Suppose I do tell you. What's in it for me?"

Obi didn't really know. She thought about it for a moment and then said, "Well, I guess you'll have the pleasure of being the first to tell me."

"Some pleasure," grumbled Sweetie Smoochkins, rolling her eyes.

"Oh, come on, Sweetie Smoochkins, please tell me! Please, please, please, please, please—" Just at that moment, from across the room, a girl's voice cried out: "Hey, get down from there!"

It was Rachel. She had just walked into her bedroom. She looked furious at finding the cat up on her dresser bothering Obi. (There was a reason why Obi loved her adopted mother as much as she did.) Startled, Sweetie Smoochkins let out a frightened meow. Whirling about, she hopped down onto the floor. As she raced past Rachel, the girl stomped her foot and said, "You know you're not supposed to be up there, you bad cat!"

Rachel came over to the dresser. Obi scampered up to her bedroom to greet her. Rachel tapped her index finger on the top of Obi's domed bedroom roof. "You okay in there, Obe?"

Obi loved it when her adopted mother called her by her nickname. Just loved it. Obe! *Obe*! It sounded so, well, loving.

Obi peered up and tried to let Rachel know through her facial expression that, yes, she was okay. She continued to gaze into Rachel's blue eyes, hoping that Rachel would tell her the big news that Sweetie Smoochkins had hinted at. But alas, Rachel said nothing more. Crossing the bedroom, she went over to her bookcase and, from one of the shelves, began to take down her music CDs.

Rachel plopped down in the middle of her floor with her music CDs. She began sorting through them, putting them in two separate piles. Obi stared at her adopted mother. What on earth was she doing? But then Obi remembered the big argument she had overheard that morning between Craig and Rachel at breakfast. The two had bickered about what music they were going to listen to in the Armstrongs' human mobile. Rachel must be picking out the CDs she wants to hear, Obi guessed.

At that moment, Mr. Armstrong came into Rachel's bedroom. He was carrying a big suitcase in one hand and several duffel bags in the other—including Rachel's blue duffel bag. This was odd. Why the suitcase and duffel bags? So far as Obi knew, the only time Rachel ever used her duffel bag was when she went on a sleepover at a friend's house.

Mr. Armstrong dropped Rachel's duffel bag on the floor beside Rachel. "What are you doing, Rach?" he asked. "I thought I asked you to start getting your stuff out that you're taking with you."

"I am," replied Rachel. "I'm picking out the music I want to listen to."

"You know what I meant," said her father. "I want you to start getting out your clothes. C'mon, Rach, we're trying to get out of here. After you pack your bag, you can go through your CDs. Put the ones you want to take with you on the kitchen table. Then I'll put them in the car for you."

"Okay," said Rachel. But she continued to sort through her CDs, as if she hadn't heard a word her father had said.

"Did you hear what I said?" asked her father.

"Yes!" groaned Rachel in a pained voice. She set her CDs on the floor beside her and picked up her duffel bag. She placed it on her lap and began to unzip it. The zipper wouldn't unzip, though.

"Argh!" she cried. "I hate this stupid zipper! Can you unzip it for me, Daddy?"

Mr. Armstrong was, by now, nearly out the door. He seemed to be in a big rush. He turned and looked at his daughter. "Come on, Rach, I've shown you before how to do it. You can figure it out for yourself."

"No, I can't!"

Mr. Armstrong suddenly became very stern. "How many times have I told you, Rachel," he said sharply, "I don't ever want to hear you say 'can't'? You're a smart kid: you *can* figure it out. Just think about it for a moment."

Rachel stared at the zipper, apparently trying to think about it. Then, as if a lightbulb had clicked on inside her brain, her face brightened as she realized that the teeth of the zipper were stuck on a piece of the duffel bag's nylon fabric. With her fingers, Rachel pulled the piece of fabric out from the zipper. This, in turn, allowed her to unzip the duffel bag.

"There, was that so hard?" asked her father.

"Yes," said Rachel.

"It was not and you know it," said her father, smiling, and he gave her an affectionate little nudge with the suitcase. He turned to leave just as Mrs. Armstrong walked into the bedroom.

"And here's your mom to help you pack," said Mr. Armstrong. With that, he stepped out the doorway and disappeared down the bedroom hallway with the suitcase and remaining duffel bags.

Mrs. Armstrong knelt down on the floor beside Rachel. Now that her father was no longer in the room, Rachel had gone back to sorting her CDs.

"What are you doing?" asked Mrs. Armstrong.

"I'm picking out the CDs I want to take with me so Daddy can put them in the car," replied Rachel.

Sometimes Rachel said or did things that truly befuddled Obi, and this, needless to say, was one of those times. Had Rachel really forgotten so soon that her father had asked her to pack her duffel bag before selecting her music CDs?

"Well, before you do that," said Mrs. Armstrong, "let's you and I pack your bag. The first order of business is underwear. Please get some out of your dresser."

Rachel rolled her eyes and heaved a huffy little sigh to let her mother know that this was not what *she* thought the first order of business should be. Rachel stepped in front of the dresser—and Obi's apartment. From her bedroom tower, Obi watched Rachel take out a pair of yellow underpants from the top drawer.

"Rachel, I think you're going to need a bit more underwear than that," said Mrs. Armstrong. "We're going on a big trip, remember?"

Obi was shocked, flabbergasted. She stared at Mrs.

Armstrong with astonishment. Did Mrs. Armstrong really say what Obi thought she had said? They were going on a *trip?!*

No, not just a trip.

A *big* trip, she had said!

chapter four Obi's Secret

Obi had a secret. Nobody knew she had a secret. Not Mack, the dog. Not Mr. Smithers, the parrot. Not Betsy and Susie, the goldfish. Not the three cats, Sugar Smacks, Honey Buns, or Sweetie Smoochkins. (Certainly not the cats!) Not Craig's pets. (How would *they* know?) Not the other members in Rachel's family. Not even Rachel herself knew that Obi had a secret. So what was the big secret?

Obi knew how to read.

Okay, you're thinking, no way, right? Gerbils can't read! But Obi could. Here's how it happened:

For as long as Obi could remember, Mr. Armstrong had read bedtime stories to Rachel. Every evening before Rachel went to bed, the two of them would make themselves comfy in the blue upholstered armchair that was in Rachel's bedroom, right beside her dresser. While

Mr. Armstrong read aloud, Rachel, dressed in her pj's, would snuggle up close to her father in such a way that she could see the pictures on the pages (or when she was older and there were few, or no, pictures, the words themselves).

Over the years that Obi had been Rachel's pet, Mr. Armstrong had read hundreds of children's books to Rachel. As Rachel grew older, Mr. Armstrong read fewer and fewer books with pictures in them and more and more chapter books.

And where was Obi while Mr. Armstrong was reading aloud to Rachel? The little gerbil was in her apartment, which, if you recall, was on Rachel's dresser—which was right next to the chair that Mr. Armstrong and Rachel were reading in. Obi had a perfect overhead view of Rachel and her father and the book that Mr. Armstrong was reading aloud. Obi could follow the words as Mr. Armstrong read. One thing led to another thing (or one word led to another word), and before Obi knew it, she had learned to read.

And that's how it happened.

So Obi was absolutely thrilled to hear about the trip. Where were they all going? A *big* trip, Mrs. Armstrong had said. Obi thought of the books that

Mr. Armstrong had read to Rachel and remembered some of the amazing places that the books had described: New York City (*Harriet the Spy*) . . . England (*Winnie-the-Pooh, Mary Poppins, Harry Potter*) . . . Florida (*Because of Winn-Dixie*) . . . Paris (*Madeline*) . . . the Dakota Territory (*Little House on the Prairie*) . . . Detroit (*The Watsons Go to Birmingham*) . . . Oregon (*Ramona*) . . .

Could it be Obi was actually going to *see* one of these exotic places? That would be so *cool*! "Cool" was a favorite expression of Rachel's. She said it whenever she got really excited about something.

The truth was, Obi had never been on a trip before. Well, unless you counted driving home from the pet store a trip. Or that time Rachel was in second grade and she took Obi to school as her show-and-tell.

Obi watched as Rachel and her mother packed Rachel's duffel bag. The little gerbil could hardly keep still, she was so excited. In addition to underwear, Rachel and her mother packed all sorts of Rachel's things. Long pants. Several pairs of shorts. Two swimsuits. A sweatshirt. T-shirts. Socks. Pj's. Hair ties. A comb. Toothbrush.

Obi was desperate to find out more about the trip. But who could she ask?

Mack, that's who! Mack *had* to know something! The old yellow Labrador hung out in the TV room—where lots of family discussions took place. He must know all about the trip. There was only one problem. To talk to Mack, it meant Obi needed to go downstairs. And to go downstairs, it meant Obi needed to get into her Gerbil Mobile. And to get into her Gerbil Mobile, it meant Obi needed to get Rachel to take her out of her apartment and place her inside the Gerbil Mobile.

chapter five

A Two-Step Process

Actually, getting Rachel to take Obi out of her apartment wasn't quite as difficult as you might think. That's because, during the time she'd been Rachel's pet, Obi had devised a rather clever method of getting Rachel to put her into her Gerbil Mobile. It consisted of a two-step process that involved (1) Obi's exercise wheel, and (2) the front bars of Obi's apartment.

As luck would have it, just at that moment, the twins, Betsy and Susie, came bursting into the room, squabbling, all angry at each other because they both wanted to use the same pink duffel bag and neither one would let the other use it. Like so many Armstrong squabbles, Obi could not understand what all the fuss was about. Who cared which one got the pink duffel bag? They should be excited. After all, they were about to go on a trip! A *big* trip!

"Stop fighting or neither one of you will get to use that bag," said Mrs. Armstrong. Then, turning to Rachel, she said, "We're pretty much finished here. I'm going to go help the twins pack. Daddy will put your bag in the car. Before you do anything, though, I want you to make your bed, okay?"

"Okay," replied Rachel.

As Mrs. Armstrong got up to leave with the twins, Obi slipped down her tube to her living room. She hurried through the deep drifts of cedar shavings to her exercise wheel. Just as she was about to jump onto the exercise wheel and put Step One into effect, Obi happened to glance over at Rachel, who was now alone in the room. Startled, Obi stopped and stared. Rachel was not making her bed, the way her mother had asked her to. No, she had picked up her music CDs off the floor and was now heading out the door with them.

"Mom!" cried Obi. "Mom, wait, don't go!" For Obi's plan to work, she needed Rachel to stay in her bedroom.

Frantic, the little gerbil hopped onto her exercise wheel and began to run. No, not run, *sprint*! Her legs flew. This, in turn, caused her exercise wheel to spin and squeak like crazy.

Squeak! Squeak! Squeak! Squeak!

Step One, as usual, worked like a charm. Hearing the squeaky exercise wheel, Rachel stopped, turned, and gazed at Obi. Now that she had her adopted mother's attention, it was time for Step Two. Obi leaped off her exercise wheel, dashed over to the front of her apartment, opened her mouth, and began to gnaw on one of the metal bars.

"Stop it, Obe!" Rachel cried, a worried expression on her face— just as Obi had hoped. "You know how I hate when you do that! You'll break a tooth!"

But Obi kept right on gnawing. She wanted Rachel to think she was restless and desperately needed to get some exercise in her Gerbil Mobile.

"Tell you what," said Rachel as she came back to the dresser, "I'll put you in your Gerbil Mobile, how about that?"

That, of course, sounded fantastic to Obi! The front of Obi's apartment had a small square door that, like the rest of the walls of her living room, was made of bars. Rachel pulled open the door, reached in, and took Obi out. She placed Obi in the Gerbil Mobile and closed the hatch door. Then Rachel came downstairs, carrying her music CDs in one hand and Obi inside the Gerbil Mobile in the other.

When Rachel entered the kitchen, all three cats—Sugar Smacks, Honey Buns, and Sweetie Smoochkins—rushed over. Meowing, the cats rubbed their furry sides against Rachel's legs.

Rachel, who was not a cat person (thank goodness!), just ignored them. She went over to the round kitchen table and set her music CDs on the blue-and-white-checkered tablecloth. Suddenly, from upstairs, there came a shout from Mrs. Armstrong: "Rachel, where are you?"

"Downstairs," Rachel called back.

"What are you doing downstairs? I thought I asked you to make your bed! Now get up here and do it this instant!"

"Okay, okay!" said Rachel. Quickly, she left the kitchen and started up the stairs—still carrying the Gerbil Mobile!

"Hey, what about me?" cried Obi in alarm. "You forgot to put me down, Mom!"

Of course, Rachel, being human, could not understand a single one of Obi's squeaks.

Desperate, Obi broke into a furious run inside her globe.

Scratch! Scratch! Scratch!

It worked! Rachel heard the gerbil's small claws clicking and scratching against the plastic interior of the globe, and she glanced down at Obi.

"Oh!" said Rachel with a look of surprise, as if she had totally forgotten she was still carrying Obi. "Oops, sorry, Obe! Guess I forgot about you!" Rachel came back downstairs and set the Gerbil Mobile on the front hallway floor. The moment the plastic globe touched the green carpet, off Obi went in the direction of the TV room.

"**Mack! Mack!**" Obi cried excitedly as she rolled into the room where the Armstrongs watched TV. Mack lay, with his eyes closed, on his big, round, comfy-looking doggie bed that sat in the corner of the room. "I just heard the good news, Mack!"

Mack didn't open his eyes. He was sound asleep. Obi couldn't believe it. How could Mack sleep on a big day like today when they were all about to go on a big trip?

"Hawo, Mack?" said Obi as she rolled the Gerbil Mobile up to Mack's face.

"Erp! Hawo! Hawo!" shrieked a high-pitched voice from across the room.

It was the parrot, Mr. Smithers. He was perched on the trapeze bar in his wire cage, which was suspended from the ceiling.

In truth, Obi really just wanted to talk to Mack.

However, being the polite gerbil she was, she swiveled her Gerbil Mobile about to face the parrot. "Hawo to you, too, Mr. Smithers!" she said, peering up at the parrot. "And hawo to you, Betsy and Susie!"

The goldfish did not respond. They never did. True, they couldn't—they were, after all, underwater. But it seemed to Obi that they could at least swim over to the glass and make an attempt to be friendly instead of being antisocial and fluttering about inside their underwater castle.

"Hawo! Hawo!" said Mr. Smithers cheerfully.

"Hawo, Mr. Smithers!" said Obi. "Did you hear about the trip?"

"Hawo! Hawo!"

"Hawo!" said Obi.

"Erp! Hawo! Hawo!"

"Hawo, Mr. Smithers. Did you hear about the big trip we're all going on?"

"Hawo! Hawo! Erp! Hawo! Hawo!"

Obi wasn't quite sure what the matter was with Mr. Smithers, but there was definitely something wrong with him, because this was how a typical conversation with him always went. Needless to say, it did not make for a terribly engaging conversation. Obi rolled her Gerbil Mobile back to where Mack lay sleeping. She was so anxious to ask him about the trip, she rolled too fast. She was unable to stop when she got to his doggie bed. She smacked right into Mack's nose.

"Oops! Sorry, Mack!" cried Obi, horrified at what she had done.

The yellow Lab opened his eyes and gazed groggily at Obi inside the plastic globe.

"Hawo, Mack!" said Obi with a big, cheerful smile.

Mack, who was old and feeble and rather deaf, was a dog of few words. He merely grunted a hello and closed his eyes again.

"I just heard the good news!" said Obi.

That perked Mack up. He opened his eyes and said, "What good news?"

"You know," said Obi. "About the trip."

Mack sat up and eyed Obi closely. He no longer looked sleepy. "Trip? What trip?"

"You know, the *big* trip!"

From his cage across the room, Mr. Smithers began to shriek: "Big trip! Big trip! Erp, erp! Big trip! *Biiiig* trip!"

"What *big* trip?" demanded Mack, staring at Obi. To Obi's surprise, Mack did not seem to know anything about the trip. And then it occurred to Obi that of course Mack didn't know anything about the trip. Why would he? He was always sleeping, the lazy old dog.

"Didn't you hear?" said Obi. "The Armstrongs are going on a trip! A *big* trip!"

Deep furrows appeared on Mack's brow. He looked anxious and worried. "They're going on a big trip!?" he wailed. "Oh, *no!*"

"Erp! Oh, no! Oh, no!" cried Mr. Smithers as, ruffling his wings, he moved about on his trapeze bar.

Obi was startled and, frankly, rather puzzled by Mack's reaction. "But that's good news, Mack," she said. Then, with a question mark in her voice, she added, "Isn't it?"

"No, it's not good news!" said Mack gruffly, glaring at Obi as if somehow *she* were to blame. "A big trip means they're going to put me in the kennel!"

"Oh! Sorry, Mack, I didn't know," said Obi. Truth be told, Obi did not even know what a kennel was. She decided that this was probably not the best time to ask Mack about it, though. Obi was beginning to wish she had never asked Mack about the trip in the first place. Who knew it would cause such a big commotion?

Mr. Smithers certainly wasn't helping matters.

From his cage, he kept shrieking out: "Trip! Trip! Erp! Erp! Big trip! Big trip!" This only made Mack more upset.

"Trip! Trip!" he moaned, echoing Mr. Smithers. "Big trip! Big trip! Oh, I hate when the Armstrongs go on a big trip! Hate it! Hate it! *Hate it!* They haven't gone on a big trip in years! Why do they have to go on one now?"

"Big trip! Big trip!" shouted Mr. Smithers.

Mr. Smithers was really getting on Obi's nerves. If he said "Big trip! Big trip!" one more ti—

"Erp! Big trip! Big trip!"

Obi lost her temper. Whirling about, she snapped at the parrot: "Oh, for goodness' sake, Mr. Smithers, will you be quiet!"

"Erp! Quiet! Quiet!"

Just then, out in the hallway, Obi heard voices. Human voices. Human teenage boys' voices. The voices were coming toward the TV room. Obi, who was a timid creature by nature, became frightened. She quickly rolled her Gerbil Mobile behind the couch and hid out of sight.

Two teenage boys, both tanned and wearing baggy shorts, sandals, and untucked T-shirts that looked as if they were about two sizes too big for them, walked into the room. Obi, peering out from behind the couch, recognized the boys immediately. The shorter, heavier, pimplier of the two—the one with the shoulder-length, wavy brown hair and the T-shirt that said GOT SOCCER? across the front—was Rachel's older brother, Craig. The other boy was wearing an orange T-shirt that said LIFE IS GOOD. This boy had wild, frizzy brown hair and was wearing a red bandanna tied on his head. He also had small white earphones plugged into his ears. The earphones had a white wire connected to them that fell across the front of the boy's T-shirt and disappeared into one of the front pockets of his baggy shorts. This boy was Craig's best friend, Tad. He and Craig hung out together. From her apartment, Obi often saw the two boys walk past Rachel's bedroom doorway on their way to and from Craig's bedroom, which was down the hallway.

"Mack gets fed twice a day," said Craig. "Once in the morning and once at the end of the day."

"What about walking him?" asked Tad.

"Yeah, you'll need to walk him, too," replied Craig. "Don't worry—it's all written down on the instructions that are on the kitchen table."

As Obi listened to the boys' conversation, she glanced over at Mack. It was the most amazing thing. The wrinkled, deeply worried expression on the old dog's face had vanished. He was now practically beaming with joy. Evidently, something Craig or Tad—or both—had said had cheered up the old yellow Lab. But what?

Tad squatted in front of the dog. "Hey, Mackie boy!" he said, grinning, as he rubbed the dog behind his ears.

Mack's eyes shone brightly as he gazed into Tad's face and thumped his tail upon the floor.

Tad rose to his feet and said, "How about Mr. Smithers? How often does he get fed?"

"Once a day," replied Craig.

As Craig explained how much to feed Mr. Smithers,

Tad stepped in front of Mr. Smithers's cage and gazed in at the parrot. "Hellooo, Mr. Smithers!" he said, making his voice sound all weird and funny, like a voice in a cartoon.

"Hellooo, Mr. Smithers! Hellooo, Mr. Smithers!" replied the parrot idiotically.

It was such a shame, thought Obi, that the ability to actually speak Human should be wasted on a creature like Mr. Smithers.

"Mr. Smithers's food is here by the fish stuff," said Craig, walking over to the table on which the fish aquarium sat. He picked up a small canister  of fish food that was beside the aquarium. "As for the fish," he continued, "you just need to sprinkle some of this stuff on their water."

"Got it," said Tad. He came over and tapped his finger on the aquarium glass to try and get Betsy and Susie to swim out of their underwater castle. (Good luck, thought Obi.) "And what about Mack?" asked Tad. "Where's his food kept?"

"In the kitchen. Here, c'mon, I'll show you," said Craig, and the two boys left the room.

What was *that* all about? Obi wondered as she emerged from her hiding spot behind the couch.

"Did you hear that?" cried Mack excitedly, glancing over at Obi.

"Hear that! Hear that!" repeated Mr. Smithers.

"I'm not being put in a kennel!" said Mack. He lifted his gaze toward the ceiling and happily cried out, "Thank the Lord!"

"Thank the Lord! Thank the Lord!" cried the parrot.

Obi was now more curious—and bewildered—than ever. Anxious to hear more of the boys' conversation, she rolled her Gerbil Mobile out into the hallway. The boys weren't there. Obi heard their voices in the kitchen. She rolled her Gerbil Mobile down the hallway and stopped it just before reaching the kitchen doorway. Being ever so careful not to be seen, she peeked around the corner.

Craig and Tad were standing just outside the pantry. Obi gasped, horrified at what Tad was doing. He had Sugar Smacks, Honey Buns, and Sweetie Smoochkins cradled in his arms. Obi had never seen a human hold all three cats at the same time. As if that wasn't disturbing enough, Tad was cuddling the cats close to his face like they were cute, adorable human babies.

"Ugh!" murmured Obi, cringing.

Craig stepped into the pantry, disappearing from Obi's view. "Mack's dog food is right here," he said. "He gets a scoop of dry dog food, plus a half can of this stuff."

"How about the cats?" asked Tad, who remained in the kitchen. He pressed his nose into Sweetie Smoochkins's furry face. (This was just too much for Obi. She had to look away, she was so repulsed.) "What do I feed them?"

"They each get dry cat food and a can of this," said Craig's voice from inside the pantry. Craig went into detail on what had to be done to feed the cats. "But like I say, it's all written down in the instructions." He stepped out of the pantry and back into Obi's view. He gestured toward the Armstrongs' round kitchen table.

Tad set the cats down on the floor and leaned forward to take a look at the sheet of instructions that lay on the table, weighted down by a salt and a pepper shaker. His gaze fell upon the stack of music CDs that Rachel had placed on the table.

"Eeeewwww!" said Tad, frowning, a disgusted look on his face, like someone who had just smelled a terribly foul odor. *"Whose* music is this?"

"Not mine!" said Craig in case there was any suspicion in Tad's mind. "They're Rachel's CDs."

Tad picked up the CDs and began shuffling through them. "Oh, man, how can she listen to this stuff?"

Suddenly, before Craig had a chance to respond, Tad dropped the CDs on the table as if they'd just turned scalding hot. Taking a step back, he lifted his hands toward Rachel's CDs and made a cross sign with his two index fingers, the way Obi had once seen a man on TV do to fend off a bloodthirsty vampire. Clearly, Tad did not think much of Rachel's taste in music.

"Hey, I have to listen to this garbage while we're driving," grumbled Craig. "Rachel's taking them on the trip. That's why they're on the table. She probably put them there for my dad to put in the car."

"Why do *you* have to listen to them?" asked Tad. "Just put on your earphones and crank up the volume. You won't hear a thing."

Craig shook his head. "My dad says I can't bring my iPod or earphones or anything."

Tad stared at Craig. "Why not?"

"He says he doesn't want me tuning everyone out while we're on vacation."

"What's his problem?" exclaimed Tad.

Craig shrugged. He looked miserable.

"Well, you can't listen to this music, that's for sure," said Tad, gesturing toward Rachel's CDs. "Do you know what this music will do to you? You'll be totally brain-dead by the time you get home from your trip. You'll be walking around like a zombie, with a blank look in your eyes and drool hanging out of your mouth."

Craig did not look amused.

"Listen, there's got to be something we can do," said Tad. He began drumming his fingertips on his chin like he was deep in thought. Then, all of a sudden, his face brightened. "Okay, I know what we can do!"

"What?"

"We can hide Rachel's CDs so your dad doesn't put them in the car. When Rachel sees her CDs aren't on the table, she'll think your dad packed them. By the time she finds out he didn't, you guys will be too far into your trip to turn back." Tad placed a hand on Craig's shoulder and looked Craig straight in the eye. Speaking in a low, solemn, manly voice, Tad continued, "Your job, Craig Michael Armstrong, is to distract your sister, make sure she doesn't ask about them before you get on the Merritt Parkway. If I know your father the way I think I know your father, he won't turn back once you're on the highway."

Craig did not laugh. Didn't even smile. "It won't work," he said.

Tad looked offended. "Why won't it?"

"Because it won't," said Craig. "It'll only get me in trouble. My dad will kill me when he finds out I hid Rachel's CDs."

"But you didn't hide them," said Tad.

"Doesn't matter. I'll still get in trouble."

"That's only because I haven't finished telling you the rest of my plan," said Tad. "After you guys leave, I'll take the CDs out of the cabinet and put them back on the kitchen table. When you guys return from your trip, the CDs will be sitting right out in the open—like someone forgot to put them in the car. That someone being—"

"My *dad*!" exclaimed Craig, his eyes lighting up.

Tad, all smiles, and with a devilish gleam in his eyes, nodded. "So is that a brilliant idea or what?"

"Tad, you're a genius!"

"Yeah, I know, I know," Tad admitted. "Too bad nobody else has figured that out yet."

From her hiding spot in the hallway, Obi didn't

think Tad was a genius. She thought Tad was an absolute villain. And Craig was just as bad. How could he do such a thing to Obi's dear adopted mother, his own flesh-and-blood sister? Obi watched in disbelief as Tad put his evil plan into action. He picked up Rachel's CDs, stepped over to the stove, and put them in the cabinet that was above the stove fan, where all the cookbooks were kept.

"Of all the dirty tricks!" Obi murmured.

Obi didn't know what to do. She wanted to tell Rachel about this sinister plot, but since Obi didn't speak Human (and Rachel didn't speak Gerbil), how could she do that? Still, being the dutiful daughter that she was, Obi felt she had to at least try and warn Rachel. Obi started to roll her Gerbil Mobile around to go find Rachel when, behind her, she heard a female voice.

"Well, well, well! Snooping, are we?"

chapter Eight Gerbil Ping-Pong

Obi had never been so startled. She leaped high into the air—so high, in fact, she nearly banged her head on the top of the plastic globe. She whirled about. Honey Buns, the fluffy honey-colored cat, was sitting on the plush hallway carpet, with an amused grin on her face.

"Oh! Hawo, Honey Buns!" cried Obi. "I didn't see you there!"

"You're lucky you're in that bubble, because if you weren't you'd be in my tummy right now," said the cat.

"Or mine!" said another feline female voice, farther down the hallway.

It was Sugar Smacks, the tiger cat. She had just strolled out from the dining room.

"I guess I am rather lucky, aren't I?" said Obi. It sounded like a snide remark, but Obi didn't mean it as one. She was just nervous and flustered.

"Yeah, lucky you!" said Honey Buns. Then she did a very startling thing. With her left front paw, she swatted the Gerbil Mobile. This sent the plastic globe whizzing down the hallway toward Sugar Smacks.

"WhooooOOOaaa!" cried Obi as she frantically tried to run backward to slow down the Gerbil Mobile.

Sugar Smacks stepped in front of the Gerbil Mobile and, with her right front paw, smacked the plastic globe, sending it—and Obi—back toward Honey Buns.

Honey Buns banged the Gerbil Mobile right back to Sugar Smacks. Then Sugar Smacks smashed it back to Honey Buns. Back and forth Obi went, from one cat to the other. It was as if the two cats were playing Ping-Pong, with the Gerbil Mobile as an enormous Ping-Pong ball.

Suddenly, as Obi was hurtling down the hallway toward Honey Buns, something on the stairs caught the cat's eye, startling her. She abruptly turned and dashed into the kitchen. Obi, curious, glanced up the stairs— just in time to see the brown bottom of a man's size 11 sneaker coming straight at her.

Bam!

Obi felt a tremendous jolt as the sneaker struck the Gerbil Mobile. The next thing Obi knew, she was flopping about inside the Gerbil Mobile as it rocketed down the hallway toward the old grandfather clock that stood near the front door. The plastic globe crashed into the bottom of the antique clock and finally, mercifully, came to a stop.

Dizzy, her eyes all out of focus, Obi got to her feet. She peered down the hallway. Something tall and blurry stood at the bottom of the stairs. As Obi's vision came into focus, she saw, to her horror, that it was Mr. Armstrong. He stood there, glaring at Obi, his hands full. He was carrying Rachel's blue duffel bag, a white canvas bag overflowing with folded beach towels, and other bags and items.

"Oh, for crying out loud!" Mr. Armstrong bellowed. "Rachel, get down here *now*!"

Rachel appeared at the top of the stairs. She looked timid and worried. She could tell by the tone of her father's voice that he was not happy. "Yes, Daddy?"

"I nearly tripped and broke my neck on Obi's darn bubble! Please put him back in his cage! C'mon, Rach, we're about to leave! I want you to use the bathroom, and then go wait in the car."

Rachel hurried down the stairs and swept the Gerbil Mobile up in her hands. "Come on, Obi!" she said. She sounded annoyed. She carried the Gerbil Mobile back up to her bedroom.

In her bedroom, Rachel took Obi out of the plastic bubble and held the little gerbil in her palm. Obi stared up into her adopted mother's face. She wanted so desperately to tell her that (a) it wasn't Obi's fault that Rachel's father almost tripped and broke his neck on the Gerbil Mobile, and (b) Craig and Tad had just committed the most sinister crime against her.

If only I could speak Human!, thought Obi for about the one hundred millionth time in her life.

Rachel opened the door to Obi's apartment and plopped her down on the cedar shavings in her living room. Closing the apartment door, Rachel said, "Bye, Obi."

Obi, blinking, stared at Rachel as she walked out of her bedroom. The little gerbil was completely baffled.

Bye, Obi?

Obi had no idea what was happening, but she had an awful feeling that whatever it was was not a good thing. She sat, bewildered, in her living room, trying to make sense of what had just happened. In her mind, she kept hearing Rachel's last two words to her. They sounded so ominous!

Bye, Obi.

Outside the house, Obi heard human voices. Then she heard the *thunk!* of a door being closed on a human mobile. Obi darted into her tube and scrambled up to her bedroom. Lifting herself onto her hind legs, she peered out of Rachel's bedroom window.

The Armstrongs' human mobile, a big, dark, hulking vehicle, was parked in the asphalt driveway. A luggage carrier, long and black and boxy, sat atop the roof. It was open—Mr. Armstrong stood beside the human mobile, putting bags and suitcases into the elongated box. He stuck some folding beach chairs and a collapsed beach umbrella in and then closed the top of the luggage carrier.

"All right, we're out of here!" Mr. Armstrong declared triumphantly, like this was a huge accomplishment.

He and the other Armstrongs climbed into the Armstrongs' human mobile. Meanwhile, Craig's friend, Tad, stood in the driveway, holding a skateboard under his arm.

"Have a good trip!" Tad cried as he waved to Craig and the Armstrongs. They all waved back and said goodbye, and Mrs. Armstrong told Tad to be sure to call if anything should happen or if he had any questions.

"If you forgot anything, just call," said Tad.

"If we forgot anything, we'll just do without it," replied Mr. Armstrong.

Obi noticed Tad and Craig exchange a furtive, conspiratorial glance. Then Tad dropped his skateboard onto the driveway and hopped onto it. Pushing off with his foot, he rolled down the driveway, then down the street.

By now, the Armstrongs were all in their human mobile, with their doors closed and their seat belts buckled. Seated in the driver's seat, Mr. Armstrong started up the motor of the human mobile.

Obi became alarmed. "Wait! *Wait!*" she cried. "What are you doing? You can't go! You don't have *me!*"

Obi watched in horror as the Armstrongs' human mobile began to back out of the driveway. "The Armstrongs are leaving without me!" she exclaimed.

And then a curious thing happened.

Rachel, who was seated with the twins in the second-row backseat (Craig was all by himself in the third-row backseat), leaned forward and said something to her father. What was Rachel saying? Whatever her adopted mother was saying, she looked very earnest and concerned.

Mr. Armstrong stopped backing up the human mobile. He closed his eyes, made a pained face, then opened his eyes. With a look of total exasperation, he drove back up the driveway. He stopped the vehicle, leaving the motor running. The back door flung open and Rachel leaped out. Mrs. Armstrong, seated in the front passenger seat, also stepped out. Mrs. Armstrong had keys in her hand. Rachel and her mother walked quickly toward the kitchen entrance of the Armstrongs' house.

Obi's heart leaped with joy. Obviously, at the very last moment, Rachel had remembered Obi. Wasn't that just like her adopted mother? Obi was so glad Rachel had remembered her in the nick of time.

From the human mobile, Mr. Armstrong stuck his head out of his window and impatiently yelled, "Make it snappy!"

Don't worry, Mr. Armstrong, thought Obi. *I'll* be snappy!

Obi zipped down her tube to her living room so she'd be all ready when Rachel came into the bedroom to get her.

Downstairs, Obi heard a key turn in the kitchen door. Then she heard Mack bark in the TV room and then the sound of the wooden door being pushed open. She waited for the sound of Rachel's footsteps bounding up the stairs.

Obi waited and waited, but, strangely, she heard no sound of footsteps hurrying up the stairs. In fact, to Obi's surprise, she heard nothing. Nothing at all!

What was going on? What could Rachel and her mother possibly be doing downstairs?

And then Obi heard a terrible sound: the sound of

the kitchen door closing. Then an even worse sound: that of a key turning in the lock.

What was going on? Obi rushed back up to her bedroom and peered out Rachel's bedroom window. Down in the driveway, Rachel and her mother were climbing back into the Armstrongs' human mobile.

"No! *NO!*" cried Obi frantically. "What are you doing? You can't go! You don't have me! What about *me*!?"

Once Rachel and her mother were again in the human mobile, Mr. Armstrong backed the vehicle out into the street.

"Stop! *STOP!*" exclaimed Obi as tears slid down her furry face. "You can't go! You can't! Not without me! No, NO!"

The Armstrongs' human mobile shot forward down the street. It passed one house, then another, growing smaller and smaller as it drove farther and farther away. At the end of the street, the human mobile stopped at a STOP sign, then slipped out of view behind a large brown house that stood at the corner.

For the longest time, Obi sat in her bedroom tower, staring out of her blue plastic dome, her eyes focused on just one thing: the brown house on the corner that the Armstrongs' human mobile had vanished behind. She stared and stared at it, hoping that the Armstrongs' human mobile would reappear from behind the house. It just had to, she told herself. Obi refused to believe that Rachel would simply abandon her like this.

She couldn't! She wouldn't!

It was the oddest thing, but as Obi was gazing out of Rachel's bedroom window, she had the eeriest feeling that she was being observed. To be honest, this was not an entirely new sensation. There were many times when Obi was in her apartment that she thought she was being secretly watched. But she felt it much more keenly now. She turned and glanced about Rachel's bedroom. Nobody was there. Nobody was out in the bed-room hallway, either—at least that part of the hallway that Obi could see.

Obi turned back to stare out the window. It was a beautiful day, with lots of summery blue sky and billowy puffs of white clouds. It was windy, and the old Nor-way maple in the front yard was heaving about in the gusts. Over by the telephone wire that stretched from the Armstrongs' house to the wood telephone pole out by the street, a flash of gray fur caught Obi's eye. It was the gray squirrel that had a nest in the top branches of the Norway maple. He was dashing across the telephone wire. Being an indoor pet, Obi, of course, had never met this outdoor creature, but she had often watched him from Rachel's bedroom window. He was an amazingly brave fellow, this squirrel, and quite the acrobat. With his fluffy tail flicking all about, he zipped across the skinny telephone wire and then, rather unexpectedly, flung himself into the air. He didn't hesitate, didn't even pause. He just leaped off the wire and soared through the air, landing on one of the tree's branches. He contin-ued on his way, jumping from branch to branch.

Ordinarily, Obi loved to see the squirrel perform his dangerous high-wire act and then hurl himself through the air to the maple tree. But not today. Today, Obi's heart ached too much to be dazzled by the squirrel's heroics.

An hour must have passed. Then another hour. Obi continued to stare out Rachel's window. At one point, a big, hulking, dark human mobile drove around the corner of the brown house. Obi, thrilled, sprang onto her hind legs to get a better look. False alarm. It was merely another human mobile that looked like the Armstrongs'. Those darn human mobiles—they all looked alike.

Obi was starting to feel hungry. She had not eaten all day. She rose, shook off a few cedar shavings that were clinging to her fur, and dropped down her tube. She waded through the deep cedar shavings that swallowed up her living room floor. Arriving in her kitchen area, Obi stopped and stared in horror.

Her little food dish was empty. Not one seed remained. In all the excitement of that morning, Rachel had forgotten to feed Obi.

Panic seized Obi. "Oh, no!" she gasped. "What am I going to do? I need food to survive!" She glanced at her water bottle hanging from the bars of her living room. It was nearly empty.

"Oh, my gosh! Oh, my gosh!" cried Obi, freaking out. "No food! No water! What am I going to do? I'll die without food and water! I don't want to *die*! I'm too young to die!"

Just then, from out in the hallway, Sugar Smacks strolled into Rachel's bedroom. For the first time in her life, Obi was actually glad to see a cat. For one thing, it meant that Obi was not the only pet that had been left behind by the Armstrongs. She hoped that Sugar Smacks might be able to tell her where the Armstrongs had gone.

Obi stepped over to the bars of her apartment. "Hawo, Sugar Smacks!" she called, smiling her most cheerful smile. "Am I glad to see *you*!"

$\mathcal{S}$ugar smacks casually ambled across the yellow carpet to Rachel's dresser. Then the cat sprang up, landing on top of the dresser, near Rachel's upturned hairbrush that the girl had forgotten to take. She plopped herself down in front of Obi's apartment, wiggled a front paw through the narrow bars of Obi's living room, and tried to swat poor Obi.

"You don't happen to know where the Armstrongs went, do you?" asked Obi, staying just out of reach of the cat's lunging paw.

"Who wants to know?" asked Sugar Smacks.

"Well . . . me," replied Obi.

"Why do you want to know?"

"Just curious."

"Tell you what," said Sugar Smacks. "We'll play a game."

"A game?" said Obi. "What kind of a game?"

"You try and touch my paw without me smacking you with my sharp claws."

This really did not sound like such a fun game to Obi. In fact, it sounded quite dangerous. "What happens if I touch your paw and I don't get mauled?" asked Obi.

"Well, if that should happen, I'll answer one of your questions," replied the cat. "What do you say?"

The truth was, Obi didn't dare say no, not to a cat. She was too afraid. Obi tried to look at the bright side. If she played the game, she might be able to find out where the Armstrongs had gone—and, more important, when they were coming home.

"Go ahead," said Sugar Smacks. "Touch my paw."

Cautiously, her heart thumping, a very nervous Obi stepped toward Sugar Smacks's paw. Obi waited for just the right moment, and then, with lightning-fast speed, she touched the furry top of the cat's paw. Quickly, Obi yanked her paw away and leaped back.

To Obi's surprise, Sugar Smacks burst into peals of shrill, uncontrollable, high-pitched giggles.

"Hee-hee-hee-hee-hee!"

It was a very unbecoming sound for a cat to make— or any creature, for that matter.

"Again!" cried Sugar Smacks gleefully, taking another swat at Obi. "Do it again!"

"But I didn't get to ask you a question," said Obi.

"Oh, all right, ask one," said Sugar Smacks. She sounded annoyed and impatient with this part of the game.

"Where did the Armstrongs go?"

"On vacation."

"Where?"

Sugar Smacks smiled and shook her head. "Uh-uh!" she said, wagging her paw at Obi as if the little gerbil was being very naughty. "You know the rules, Obi. You have to touch my paw before I answer another question."

Obi lifted her small paw and stepped forward. She waited for just the right moment, then touched the top of the cat's paw. Once again, as Obi leaped back to safety, the cat shrieked with delight. *Hee-hee-hee-hee-hee!*

"Where did the Armstrongs go on vacation?"

"A lot of places."

"What kind of places?"

The cat let out an impatient sigh. "C'mon, Obi, you know the rules."

Obi felt cheated. In her opinion, "a lot of places" was not a fair answer. But Obi was too timid to protest. She stepped forward and touched the cat's paw again.

"Hee-hee-hee-hee-hee!"

"What kind of places?"

"One of the places was called Cape Cod. Okay, touch me again!"

Obi did.

"Hee-hee-hee-hee-hee!"

"How long will the Armstrongs be gone?"

"Two weeks."

"Two weeks!" cried Obi, aghast.

"C'mon, c'mon!" cried Sugar Smacks. "You're taking too long! Touch me again!"

The game continued with Obi touching Sugar Smacks's outstretched paw, Sugar Smacks bursting into peals of giggles, Obi asking a question, Sugar Smacks answering, and then Obi touching the cat's paw again to ask another question. Obi asked all sorts of things. "Did any other pets go with the Armstrongs?" ("No.") "Who's feeding the pets while the Armstrongs are gone?" ("That Tad boy.") "Just before the Armstrongs left, Rachel and her mother came back into the house. Do you know why?" ("They came into the kitchen and Rachel wrote something on a piece of paper.")

"What did she write?" asked Obi.

Now, if Sugar Smacks had been paying more attention and not been so giggly, she might have realized how strange this question sounded. Why would Obi ask such a thing? After all, animals can't read.

"Like I can read," replied Sugar Smacks. "Go on! Touch me again!"

"But I don't have any more questions," said Obi.

"Oh, c'mon, you must have *one* more question!"

Obi didn't want Sugar Smacks to get angry, so she touched her paw again.

"Hee-hee-hee-hee-hee!"

"When is Tad coming to feed us?"

"Don't know," replied Sugar Smacks. "Touch me again! Touch me again!"

Obi really did not want to play anymore. But what could she do? As she stepped forward to touch the cat's paw, an unexpected thing happened. Sugar Smacks abruptly pulled her paw out from Obi's living room. She jerked up her head, ears perked.

"What was *that*?" she demanded.

Obi stared at her and said, "What was what?"

"That noise!"

"What noise? I didn't hear—"

And then Obi heard it. The noise came from downstairs—from in the kitchen. It was the sound of a key turning in a lock. Then there was the sound of a door being pushed opened. And then there was the sound of Mack in the living room, barking at the sound of the door being opened. His bark sounded old and feeble, not young and ferocious like an eager watchdog's.

"Must be Tad!" exclaimed Sugar Smacks.

Without saying another word, Sugar Smacks bounded onto the floor. She raced out of Rachel's bedroom and into the hallway, disappearing in the direction of the stairs that led down to the kitchen.

chapter Twelve Forgotten

Obi stood still and listened. She heard a cat meow down in the kitchen. Then she heard two other cats meow. Tad must be feeding the cats, Obi decided.

A few minutes passed. Then Obi heard the sound of human footsteps tromping up the stairs to the bedroom hallway.

Here comes Tad! thought Obi.

Obi sat up on her hind legs to greet Tad. But to Obi's great surprise, the boy walked right past Rachel's bedroom.

"Wait, Tad! I'm in here!" Obi called out.

Naturally, Tad, being human, could not hear Obi. But even if he did have the ability to hear a gerbil, chances are he still would not have heard her, because, once again, the boy had earphones plugged into his ears and was listening to his very loud music. It was so loud, in fact, that even Obi, from inside Rachel's bedroom, could hear the faint, tinny sound of a rock 'n' roll band.

Obi was dumbfounded. Why hadn't Tad come into Rachel's bedroom and fed her? Then she remembered that Craig's bedroom was just down the hallway. He must be feeding Craig's pets first. He'll stop in and feed me on his way back downstairs, she told herself.

Obi waited patiently for Tad to reappear. He sure was taking a long time. What was he doing? Suddenly, out in the hallway, Obi caught sight of the boy. She lifted herself up on her hind legs to get a better view. Once again, to Obi's astonishment, the boy walked right past Rachel's bedroom.

"Wait, Tad, where are you going?" she exclaimed. "You forgot *me*!"

What was going on? Why hadn't Tad come into Rachel's bedroom and fed her? Oh, I bet I know, thought Obi. He probably needs to get me my gerbil food from the kitchen pantry. He'll be right back.

But Tad did not come right back. What was taking the boy so long? Obi strained her ears, hoping to hear the sound of Tad's footsteps tromping up the stairs again.

Obi finally heard something, but not the sound she

was hoping to hear. Down in the kitchen, a door closed. The next thing Obi heard was a key turning, locking the door.

Obi was stunned, incredulous. Frantic, she raced up her plastic tube to her bedroom and gazed out Rachel's bedroom window. Down on the Armstrongs' driveway, Tad was hopping onto his skateboard. He rolled down the driveway and out into the street, and then, with another push of his foot, the boy coasted down the street.

"Wait, Tad! You can't go!" cried Obi. "You forgot to feed me! Come back!"

Obi burst into tears. She just sobbed and sobbed. She couldn't help it. She felt so forlorn and so forgotten. First Rachel had left her at home, and now Tad hadn't fed her. Suddenly, during a particularly heart-wrenching sob, Obi got that weird feeling again—the feeling that someone was secretly observing her. With wet, glistening eyes, she glanced about her adopted mother's bedroom. Just like before, though, she saw no one.

"Hawo?" Obi called out.

She listened, but the only sounds Obi heard were the sound of her own heartbeat, her sniffling, and the grandfather clock down in the front hallway.

Tick-tock, tick-tock . . .

chapter Thirteen Hungry

Obi had the worst time falling asleep that night. She was so hungry, all she could think about was how incredibly hungry she was. As she lay in her bedroom, nestled in a big mound of cedar shavings, she could hear her empty stomach making loud, gurgling noises. She tried not to listen, but it wasn't easy. In her mind, she kept asking herself the same questions over and over again:

Why hadn't Tad fed her? Could it be Tad thought Rachel had fed her that morning? Yes, that must be it, Obi decided. That *had* to be it. She was sure he would feed her tomorrow morning when he returned.

But there was another possible reason why Tad hadn't fed her. Obi tried not to think about this other reason, but it kept nagging at her, the same way her hungry stomach kept nagging at her.

Obi loved her adopted mother very much, but even she had to admit that Rachel had a serious shortcoming. She was always forgetting to do things. Mrs. Armstrong was constantly having to remind Rachel about something the girl had neglected to do. Like make her bed. Or pick up her clothes off the bedroom floor. Or do her homework. Or brush her teeth. ("Did you floss and use fluoride rinse? Well, young lady, go back into the bathroom and do it, please!") Or practice her violin. (To be honest, Obi really didn't mind when Rachel forgot to practice her violin. Rachel's violin playing was about as soothing to listen to as Obi's squeaky exercise wheel.) Almost every day, it seemed, Rachel had to be reminded about one thing or another.

Could it be—*no, it couldn't*—that Rachel—*no, no, no, absolutely not!*—had forgotten—*stop it, Obi, don't even go there!*—to tell Tad—*I said stop it!*—that he had to feed her?

Just thinking this caused a lump to form in Obi's throat and her eyes to well up with tears. Luckily, Obi fell asleep right about then, for the next thing she knew it was bright and early the next morning, and sunlight was streaming through Rachel's bedroom window. For a moment, Obi just sat in her bedroom, basking in the warmth of the sun. But then she heard her stomach. It was growling even louder than the night before. It felt emptier, too.

Obi climbed down her tube to her living room. She walked over to her dish, hoping it might have filled itself miraculously overnight. But alas, it had not. Obi glanced at the dollhouse refrigerator that stood in the corner of her living room. Gosh, if only it was a real fridge, stocked with all kinds of delicious gerbil food, she thought. Down by her feet, Obi spied a broken shell from a sunflower seed that she had eaten days ago. She licked the pale white inside of the shell. It bore the ever-so-faint taste of a sunflower seed. It wasn't much of a taste, but at least it was something.

Had it been an ordinary day, Obi would have hopped onto her exercise wheel and gone for a run. Today, though, Obi did not dare go for a run. She was worried exercise would only make her hungrier.

Obi sighed and plopped down in her living room. She sat facing Rachel's bedroom doorway. There was nothing else she could think of to do but to wait for Tad.

Sometime in the middle of the morning, Mack began to bark. Downstairs, Obi heard a key turn in the lock.

Then came the sound of the door being pushed open. Obi, excited, leaped to her feet.

Tad was back!

Just like the day before, Obi heard the cats meow down in the kitchen. A few minutes later, she heard Tad's footsteps clomping up the stairs. Obi eagerly sat up on her hind legs.

Obi caught sight of Tad out in the bedroom hallway. He was wearing the same clothes he had on the day before. And just like yesterday, he was wearing a red bandanna on his frizzy-haired head and had earphones plugged into his ears. And just like the day before, he was walking right past Rachel's bedroom doorway.

Obi quickly tried to catch the boy's attention. "Hawo, Tad! In here!"

Tad was munching on something. He also had things in his hand. Small, dark, round things. Cookies! They were cookies! While the Armstrongs were away, Tad was eating their cookies!

Tad was about to vanish from Obi's view when he suddenly stopped short.

"Whoa!" he blurted out.

Startled, Tad jumped back and dropped the cookies. They bounced and scattered on the hallway carpet, right in front of Rachel's bedroom doorway. Tad bent down and began picking up the cookies. He was directly in front of Rachel's bedroom doorway. Obi couldn't have asked for a better opportunity to get the boy's attention.

Obi began jumping in the air. She leaped up and down, like a bouncing ball. "Hawo, Tad!" she shouted, waving her paws. "Yoo-hoo! It's me, Obi! I'm in here!"

No luck! Tad didn't look over. Obi stopped jumping and frantically tried to think of what else she could do to get the boy to notice her. The exercise wheel! She leaped onto it and burst into a wild sprint.

Squeak! Squeak! Squeak! Squeak!

Now, Tad should have heard Obi's squeaky exercise wheel. And he would have if he hadn't had those gosh-darn earphones in his ears! All Tad could hear was his darn old music!

To Obi's dismay, Tad stood up, popped a cookie into his mouth, and continued on his way down the hallway toward Craig's bedroom, disappearing from Obi's view.

Obi stopped running. She was gasping for breath.

"Tad, come back!" she called out. "I'm in here! Don't go! You have to come back and feed me!"

Ten agonizing minutes later, Tad reappeared in the hallway. But just like before, he walked right past Rachel's bedroom and down the stairs.

Obi felt so sad and sorry for herself. She also felt lots hungrier from running so hard on her exercise wheel. And weaker, too. She heard the door down in the kitchen close, lock. Obi lost it then. With a loud, mournful wail, she broke into sobs.

A half hour or so later, Obi was still sobbing away when Sugar Smacks strolled into Rachel's bedroom licking her lips of whatever tasty morsel Tad had fed her for breakfast that morning.

Sugar Smacks hopped up onto Rachel's dresser and peered in at Obi. "What's your problem?" she asked.

"Tad didn't feed me!" blubbered Obi.

"Too bad," said Sugar Smacks as she wiggled her left front paw through the bars of Obi's living room. She didn't sound terribly sympathetic, though. "Hey, let's play our game!"

Our game? You mean, *your* game! Obi wanted to say. But Obi could never say such a thing. Not to Sugar Smacks.

"C'mon, c'mon, I don't have all day," said Sugar Smacks impatiently. "Don't you have any questions?"

Of course Obi had questions. Plenty of questions. Like why wasn't Tad feeding her? Obi lifted her paw, stepped forward, and tapped Sugar Smacks on her paw.

The cat, all giddy, burst into hysterical giggles. *"Hee-hee-hee-hee-hee!"*

"Did Tad feed all the other Armstrong pets?" asked Obi.

"Yup," replied Sugar Smacks.

Obi was sorry she asked. It only made her feel worse.

"How come Tad didn't feed me?"

"Aren't you forgetting something?" asked Sugar Smacks.

"Oh, sorry," said Obi. She reached over and touched Sugar Smacks's paw.

"Hee-hee-hee-hee-hee!" the tiger cat giggled loudly.

"How come Tad didn't feed me?" Obi asked again.

"Don't know," replied Sugar Smacks. "C'mon, c'mon! You're taking too long! You're not very good at this game, are you?"

As Sugar Smacks was saying this, a voice in the

doorway suddenly said, "There you are, Sugar Smacks! I was wondering where you had disappeared to!"

It was Honey Buns. In a flash, Sugar Smacks yanked her paw out from Obi's apartment and jumped down to the floor. Clearly, Sugar Smacks did not want Honey Buns to find out about their game. Apparently, she was worried that if Honey Buns got wind of it, she'd want to butt in and play, too.

"What were you doing up there?" asked Honey Buns with a glance up toward Obi's apartment.

"Nothing!"

"It didn't look like nothing."

"No, really, it was nothing," insisted Sugar Smacks.

"Oh, c'mon, you can tell me."

"There's nothing to tell!"

"You never tell me anything!" said Honey Buns, pouting.

"That's not true!" replied Sugar Smacks. "And just to show you, come with me. You've got to see this hairball that I spit up this morning. It's humongous!"

"Yeah? Really?" said Honey Buns, instantly cheering up. "Where is it? Show me! Show me!"

With that, the two cats trotted out of Rachel's bedroom.

Alone, Obi crawled up her tube to her bedroom and flopped down onto the cedar shavings. She had never felt so desolate in all her life. What was Obi to do? She needed food and water to survive. The Armstrongs were going to be gone for two weeks.

"Two weeks!" wailed Obi.

And then, for what seemed like the millionth time since Rachel had left, Obi burst into tears.

chapter fourteen

The Gray Squirrel

A day passed. Or was it two? Or three? Obi was so hungry and weak, she lost track. Each morning and evening, Tad came to feed the Armstrongs' pets. But he never fed Obi. Never once did he even glance into Rachel's bedroom on his way to feed Craig's pets. Obi tried several more times to make noises to get Tad's attention, but the teenager was always listening to music on his earphones and never heard her. So, finally, Obi gave up. It got to the point where she was worried that if she overexerted herself too much, she might collapse from hunger.

Obi tried to keep a positive attitude. She wondered what her namesake, Obi-Wan Kenobi, would do in such a situation. If I was a fearless, clever, and resourceful Jedi knight, thought Obi, what would I do?

She heaved a forlorn sigh. "Who am I kidding? I'm

no Jedi knight! I'm just a little gerbil in a pathetic little cage who's very, very hungry!" Her bottom lip trembled as she said this to herself. She had never called her apartment a "cage" before. But now, to her, that was exactly what it was—just a cage.

And then one morning after Tad had come and gone, a very hopeful thing happened. Obi was in her bedroom, gazing out her bedroom window—and out Rachel's bedroom window—trying to preserve what little strength she had left, when she spotted the gray squirrel. He was outside on the Armstrongs' shingled roof, just a few yards away, poking his nose about in some dry leaves in the gutter. As Obi watched the squirrel, a thought popped into her head.

"I may not be a fearless, clever, and resourceful Jedi knight," she said to herself, "but I know someone who is!"

Obi scrambled down her tube to her living room and pressed her face against the bars on the back of her cage, near where Rachel had left her bedroom window open a crack. Cupping her front paws around her mouth, Obi shouted, "Hawo, Mr. Squirrel!"

The squirrel had discovered an acorn among the brown, brittle leaves that clogged the gutter. He was nibbling on it. Hearing Obi's voice, the squirrel jerked his head up, startled. With a perplexed, quizzical expression on his face, he glanced all about, trying to figure out who had called to him.

"Over here!" shouted Obi, waving her paw.

The squirrel lifted his eyes to Rachel's bedroom window and saw Obi. Obi expected the squirrel to hurry right over, but he didn't.

"Could you please come here?" cried Obi, smiling. "I need to talk with you for a moment!"

To Obi's surprise, the squirrel hesitated, as if he was afraid to get near Obi. This was odd. Here was this unbelievably brave and courageous Jedi knight of a creature who thought nothing of risking his life by dashing across a skinny telephone wire or leaping about in tree branches, and he was worried about coming close to Obi, a mere gerbil? At last, the squirrel put aside his reservations and ventured up the sloped roof to Rachel's bedroom window. His fluffy, feathery tail twitched nervously as he peered in through the screen at Obi.

"Hawo, my name is Obi," said Obi. "I need your help."

"What are you in for?" asked the squirrel.

"What am I *what*?" asked Obi, puzzled.

"What are you in for? Why did they lock you up?"

"What are you talking about?" asked Obi. Her eyes fell upon the acorn that the squirrel had clutched in his paws. Obi had never eaten an acorn before. She wondered what it tasted like.

"Why are you in jail?" asked the squirrel.

"Jail!?" cried Obi, staring into the squirrel's face. "I'm not in jail!" She was horrified that the squirrel would even *think* such a thing.

"C'mon," said the squirrel. "You can level with me. What did you do? Murder someone?"

cage = jail

"Absolutely not!"

"What then?"

"I didn't do anything!"

"All right, don't tell me," said the squirrel. "How long you in for?"

"Look, I'm not in jail!" said Obi. "This is my cage!"

From the look on the squirrel's face, Obi could almost hear what the squirrel was thinking: cage = jail.

"Cage and jail are not the same thing!" protested Obi.

"Sure, whatever you say," said the squirrel.

"They're not!"

"So why do you want my help?" asked the squirrel. And then, before Obi had a chance to respond, the squirrel's eyes narrowed as he put two and two together. "Oh, I get it! You want me to help you bust out, don't you?"

"No, I don't!" said Obi. "I just want your help getting me food!"

"But if I do that," said the squirrel, "I'll be aiding and abetting a criminal!"

"I'm not a criminal!"

The squirrel gave Obi the most skeptical look.

"I'm not!"

"Well, I'm not going to help you," said the squirrel. "I'm not going to end up like my poor uncle Leroy."

"Why, what happened to your uncle Leroy?" asked Obi.

"He was captured."

"Captured? By whom?"

"By the man who lives in *this* house."

Obi was stunned. "Mr. Armstrong? How did he capture your uncle Leroy?"

"In a trap. He set it outside the cellar door. Luckily for my uncle Leroy, it was one of those traps that captures the animal alive."

"What did Mr. Armstrong do with your uncle?" asked Obi.

"Nobody knows. He took him away. Uncle Leroy has never been seen or heard from since."

"Look," said Obi. "I'm sorry about your uncle Leroy. Really, I am. And trust me, I don't want you to do anything that'll get you into trouble. But I really need to eat. All I ask is that you let me have a little piece of that acorn. You can stick it through this little hole." Obi pointed to a small hole in the window screen. Rachel had made the hole with a pencil when she was about five years old, long before Obi's time.

The squirrel shook his head. "I'm sorry," he said. "But I can't help a criminal. I don't want to end up in a cage like you. A life of crime may be fine for you, Obi, but it isn't the life for me."

Before Obi could say another word, the squirrel popped the acorn back into his mouth, causing his cheeks to puff out. Then he spun about and darted down the slanted, shingled roof. When he got to the edge of the roof, the squirrel took a flying leap off the gutter. He landed onto the telephone wire. As Obi watched the squirrel race across the wire, she realized that this death-defying squirrel, whom she had thought was so brave and courageous, wasn't so brave or courageous at all. No, he was just plain daffy! When the squirrel got to the wood telephone pole, he sprang onto the wire that stretched above the street. As Obi watched him whisk across this wire, she realized that the squirrel—this creature whom she had placed so much hope in—was not going to be her Jedi knight and rescue her after all.

chapter fifteen Freedom!

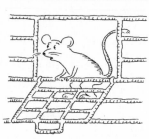

Obi felt more dejected than ever. She had put all her hopes on the squirrel courageously rescuing her from her perilous situation. What a big letdown *he* was! Obi had never felt so cheated, so hungry, so lonely, so sad and desolate. Her whole life had been turned upside down, and she had no idea how to turn it right side up.

Obi thought if she took a little nap she might feel better when she awoke, so she closed her eyes.

As it turned out, the nap was *not* a good idea. She had a nightmare, a bad one. The dream started out pleasantly enough. She dreamed that Rachel was home again. She was sitting on her bedroom floor, trying to open her blue duffel bag. Mr. Armstrong was in the dream, too. He was standing over his daughter as she tried and tried to unzip her duffel bag. She was having trouble getting it to zip open.

"I hate this stupid zipper!" cried Rachel. "Can you do it for me, Daddy?"

"C'mon, Rach, you can figure it out for yourself," said her father.

"No, I can't!" said the girl.

"How many times have I told you, Rachel, I don't ever want to hear you say 'can't'?" replied her father. "You're a smart kid: you *can* figure it out. You just need to think about it."

And then the dream got really weird. Rachel vanished, and suddenly Obi was in the dream with Mr. Armstrong.

"Can you feed me, Mr. Armstrong?" asked Obi, peering timidly up at the man, who towered over her.

"C'mon, Obi, you can figure it out for yourself," said Mr. Armstrong, talking to Obi the way he had spoken to Rachel.

"No, I can't!" cried Obi.

"How many times have I told you, Obi, I don't ever want to hear you say 'can't'?" said Mr. Armstrong. "You're a smart gerbil: you *can* figure it out. You just need to think about it."

At this point, Obi, thank goodness, woke up. She was trembling and all in a sweat. What a nightmare!

She did not like being scolded by Mr. Armstrong. Who would? Yet her dream did make Obi realize something important—that maybe she shouldn't just give up.

Obi crawled down her tube and sat down in her living room to wait for Tad.

By and by, the sunlight in Rachel's bedroom turned a rosy sunset-red, and the shadows cast by the furniture in Rachel's room grew long. The afternoon was drawing to a close. Down in the TV room, Mack began to bark. Obi sat up and listened. She heard a key turn in a lock, then the kitchen door push open. A moment later, the cats began to meow down in the kitchen. A few minutes later, Obi heard footsteps clomping up the stairs.

Obi was now on her feet, and ready. The moment Tad appeared in the hallway, Obi sprang high into the air—higher than she had ever leaped before. She waved her paws frantically about as she tried to get Tad's attention.

"Hawo, Tad!" she called out. "Taaad!"

But darn it all, Tad was wearing those earphones again. He didn't even glance into Rachel's bedroom. Just as Tad was vanishing from the doorway, Obi, in desperation, flung herself against the front of her cage.

The most startling thing happened. When Obi's

body smacked against the door of her cage, her weight caused the little square door to swing open!

Obi fell backward into her living room, softly landing on top of the cedar shavings. For several moments, she lay on her back, blinking, as she stared in astonishment at her wide-open cage door.

Oh, no! thought Obi. *Now* look what I've done! I've broken my cage! Wait till Mom comes home! I'm going to be in so much trouble!

But as Obi stared, she realized that *this* was how her cage door opened! Whenever Rachel put her hand into Obi's cage, she had to *pull* open the door. Obi was thunderstruck. To think that all this time she merely had to give the door a good push and it would open! Who knew?

Obi scrambled to her feet. Standing on her hind legs, she cautiously poked her head out the square opening of her cage, sniffed, and then pulled herself up through the doorway. She hopped down onto the surface of Rachel's dresser. She had never been outside her cage before except in the Gerbil Mobile or when she was being held by Rachel. It felt so strange. Obi walked over to her adopted mother's upturned hairbrush and sniffed it. Oh, it smelled wonderful! Just like Rachel! Then she wandered over to Rachel's school photo. It was such a comfort to see Rachel's freckled face, smiling so radiantly. It reminded Obi of happier times.

Obi went to the front of the dresser and stood close to the edge. How was she going to get down? It was much too high to jump. Glancing about, Obi spied the electrical cord of the lamp that sat on the dresser. The cord dropped down over the side to the floor. Obi went over to it, grabbed the cord in her paws, and began to lower herself down.

So *this* is what freedom feels like! thought Obi a few moments later as she trotted across the yellow shag carpet of her adopted mother's bedroom, heading for the doorway.

chapter sixteen

Craig's Bedroom

Stepping out into the hallway, Obi turned in the direction that Tad had disappeared. But Tad was nowhere in sight.

He must be in Craig's bedroom, Obi decided. The little gerbil scurried down the carpeted hallway toward Craig's bedroom, sniffing curiously and feeling strange as anything at being able to wander about free.

Arriving at Craig's bedroom door, Obi stopped. The door was slightly ajar. Obi hesitated, not sure what to do. She had never been in Craig's bedroom before. Never! It was off-limits, forbidden. Tilting her head back, Obi peered up at the signs that plastered the outside of Craig's bedroom door. KEEP OUT! BEWARE! DANGER! HIGH VOLTAGE! STOP! NO TRESPASSING!

Signs or no signs, Obi didn't see any harm in just sticking her head into the bedroom. The thing was, she needed Tad to see her. She needed him to realize that she needed to be fed.

Nervous, her heart pounding, Obi peeked in, then took a step inside the bedroom.

"Hawo? Tad?" she called out.

The first thing that struck Obi was how dark Craig's bedroom was. And no wonder: his window shades were drawn. The next thing Obi noticed was how cluttered Craig's bedroom was. Every inch of his bedroom walls, it seemed, was covered with some sort of poster or traffic sign or photograph or painting or postcard or souvenir or knickknack that only a teenage boy would tack up on his bedroom walls. Not only that, but Craig's bedroom was a huge mess. Clothes were heaped about on the floor. And Craig had gone on vacation without even making his bed! How come Craig got away with not making his bed but Rachel got yelled at for not making hers? It didn't seem fair! Obi wondered if maybe Mrs. Armstrong didn't know Craig hadn't made his bed. Maybe the signs on Craig's door had scared Mrs. Armstrong off from entering the room and see-

ing the unmade bed. If that was the case, who could blame her?

As Obi's eyes adjusted to the darkness, she noticed something else: a long creepy rope was slithering toward her from over by the closet.

Obi let out a startled gasp. That was no rope—it was a snake: a big, colorful snake!

Ordinarily, Obi would have shrieked in terror at the sight of a snake. But the truth was, she was more shocked and, well, puzzled than frightened. Indeed, for a brief moment, she even thought she was seeing things. What on earth was a snake doing in the Armstrongs' house? And loose, no less!

The large, colorful snake slid up to Obi and was about to stop when he slid too far and accidentally banged his head on one of the bedposts on Craig's bed.

"Ouch!" he cried. "I hate when I do that!"

The snake shook his head as if bumping it on the bedpost had scrambled his brain. Collecting himself, he looked at Obi and said in a deep, smooth, velvety voice, "Hellooo!"

"Hawo," said Obi in a small, timid, nervous voice.

"What's your name?" asked the snake.

"Obi," murmured Obi.

"Oohh-bee!" said the snake, slowly and deliciously pronouncing each syllable in Obi's name. "That's a *nice* name! My name is Boa!"

"Hawo, Boa," said Obi politely. Meanwhile, Obi was thinking, *This* is Craig's pet! What kind of a boy was Craig, anyway? Who in his right mind would have a *snake* for a pet?! Obi had never seen a real live snake before. She'd only seen pictures of them in books that Mr. Armstrong had read aloud to Rachel. Snakes were always portrayed as evil and sinister. Particularly to little creatures like Obi.

Obi was growing more and more nervous with each passing second. If only she were in her Gerbil Mobile right now, safely inside a bubble of thick plastic!

"Bohh-waa . . . Oohh-bee!" said the snake. Apparently, the snake really liked how the two names sounded when spoken together, for he repeated their names several times in that deep, melodious voice of his. "Bohh-waa . . . Oohh-bee! Bohh-waa . . . Oohh-bee! Bohh-waa . . . Oohh-bee!"

Obi smiled sweetly and said, "Well, I really should be going."

"You know why Master Craig named me Boa, don't you?"

"Uh . . . no," said Obi.

"I'm a bo-waa constrictor," said the snake.

"Oh, that's nice," said Obi as, still smiling, she took a step back. "Well, as I say, I really should get going. I'm looking for Tad. You haven't seen him by any chance, have you?"

"Tad?"

"You know, Craig's friend."

"Oh, *him*," said the snake in a disdainful voice. "I believe he's in the bathroom. He's supposed to be refilling the pan of water for my aquarium. But he's taking such a long time I think he may have found the comic books that Master Craig keeps beside the toilet. You know how human boys are."

Obi did not know. But she did know this: Tad needed to have his head examined. What was he possibly thinking, letting a snake roam around Craig's room free?

"You know what?" said Obi. "I think I'll go wait for Tad outside in the hallway."

"Oh, don't go, Oohh-bee!" said the snake. "Stay a while!"

"I'd like to," said Obi, which was, of course, something of a fib. "But, well, you see, I haven't eaten in a long time and I'm very, very hungry, and I really need to find Tad as soon as possible and let him know that I exist so he'll give me some food."

"*Food!*" said the snake. "Don't even mention that word! It's a sore subject!"

"Oh, sorry," said Obi. "I didn't know."

"Do you know why it's a sore subject?" asked the snake.

"Uh . . . no."

"It's a sore subject because do you know what I get fed?"

Obi, shaking her head, took another step back.

"Dead mice!" replied the snake. "I need food, *real* food! Not dead mice! That's not what I call *real* food! Give me a *live* little mouse!"

"A *live* mouse?" blurted out Obi, horrified.

"Yes, a *live* mouse," said the snake. Eyeing Obi closely, he added, "Say, *you* sort of look like a mouse. What are you, anyway?"

"A gerbil," replied Obi. She was all set to turn and flee if the snake gave even the slightest hint that it was about to attack.

To Obi's relief, the snake did not lunge forward. He frowned and said, "Never heard of a gerbil before. Boy, you sure look like a mouse! Anybody ever tell you how much you look like a mouse?"

"No," said Obi, which was the truth.

"Gosh, the resemblance is uncanny," said the snake, shaking his head in amazement.

"Well, Boa," said Obi, "I really should get going. It was nice to meet you!"

And so saying, Obi spun about and began to hurry toward the slanted ray of hallway light that fell across the bedroom floor from the slightly ajar door. Obi had taken only a few steps when suddenly, out of nowhere, this thing—this large, black, hairy, multilegged creature—sprang out and plopped down on the carpet in front of Obi.

"Eeeeek!" shrieked Obi, leaping back.

It was a spider, a large, black, hairy, eight-legged arachnid!

"**N**ot so fast, señorita!" the spider said to Obi, speaking with a Spanish accent. Then to the snake, the spider said, "You dimwit! You're letting a perfectly good meal get away!"

The snake slithered up to Obi and the spider. "A meal?" he said, puzzled. "What are you talking about, José?"

The spider lifted a leg and gestured toward Obi. *"Hollaaah!"* he said. "This creature could be *your* dinner."

"Oohh-bee?" said the snake, staring at the little gerbil in surprise. "But Oohh-bee is a gerbil."

The spider groaned and rolled his eyes. For a moment, it looked as if it was all he could do to restrain himself from reaching over with two of his eight legs and grabbing the snake by the head and shaking some brains into him. "Excuse me," said the spider. "But the last time I looked, gerbils and mice are practically the same thing!"

The snake widened his eyes in amazement. "Get out! Is that right?" He shook his head in wonder and continued, "You know, I thought Oohh-bee looked like a mouse. Didn't I say that, Oohh-bee?"

"Yes, you did," admitted Obi.

"See!" declared the snake with a triumphant grin.

The spider rolled his eyes again and muttered something under his breath about dunderheads. Obi focused her eyes on the spider and said, "Who are you?"

"He's a spider," said the snake.

"Tarantula," corrected the spider.

"A *tarantula*?" cried Obi, aghast, leaping back.

"The name is José," said the tarantula, sticking a leg out for Obi to shake. "Glad to meet you, señorita."

Obi did not shake the tarantula's leg. "Why aren't you in your cage?"

"That Tad kid lets us out whenever he comes to feed us," said the tarantula. "Before he leaves, he puts us back in our cages."

He darn well better, thought Obi. "I can't believe Craig has a real live tarantula for a pet," she said. "Not to mention a boa constrictor!"

The tarantula stifled a snort. He looked quite

amused. "Boa constrictor?" he said with a smirk, pointing a leg at the snake. "*Him*? He's no boa constrictor!"

"He's not? But I thought . . ." Obi turned and stared at the snake. "I thought you told me you were a boa constrictor."

The snake turned to the tarantula, looking just as surprised as Obi. "I'm not?"

The tarantula chuckled. "Oh, he tells everyone he's a boa constrictor. Well, everyone being me. I'm Master Craig's other pet."

"But if you're not a boa constrictor, why is your name Boa?" Obi asked the snake.

Looking totally befuddled, the snake shrugged.

"That's his problem," said the tarantula. "Master Craig named him Boa, but he's not a boa constrictor. He's *only* a corn snake. I guess Master Craig wanted a boa constrictor for a pet but had to settle for a measly old corn snake." The tarantula lifted a leg to the side of his mouth and, lowering his voice, said, "As a result, he's got a bit of an inferiority complex."

The snake heard him. Obi thought Boa would mind being described in this manner but, apparently, he didn't. In fact, he nodded in agreement, as if having an inferiority complex was a badge of honor. "That's what

I got!" he said. "An enfeerior complox! Right, José?"

"Yeah," said the tarantula. "So I'm helping the poor guy out." He put a comforting leg around the snake, just behind his oval-shaped head. "I'm teaching him all the tricks of the trade. You know, like how to be a predator instead of a sap."

"That's very kind of you," said Obi.

"Isn't it?" replied José, nodding, without any hint of modesty whatsoever.

"He's the best, this spider," said the snake.

"Tarantula," corrected the spider.

"Spider . . . tarantula," said the snake with a little shrug. "Same thing!"

The tarantula became very indignant. He removed his leg from the snake. "No, it is *not* the same thing!" he cried, annoyed. "Spiders are daddy longlegs and itsy-bitsy spiders. I'm a hairy, scary tarantula!"

"Yeah, but you're still a spider!" declared the snake with a loud, goofy laugh.

"Tarantula!" replied the tarantula, incensed.

"Spider!"

"Tarantula!"

Hearing the snake and tarantula bicker, Obi got the feeling that this was not the first time that the two of them had disagreed over this subject. It also dawned on Obi that this was a perfect chance for her to escape. Slowly, so as not to arouse suspicion, the little gerbil took a step back, then another step. Then she swung about and dashed through the lighted slit in the bedroom doorway. Out in the hallway, Obi raced toward Rachel's bedroom. She was almost there when, down the hallway, who should appear walking leisurely up the carpeted stairs but Sweetie Smoochkins!

The moment Sweetie Smoochkins spotted Obi, the cat froze. The moment Obi spotted Sweetie Smoochkins, the little gerbil froze. The cat's eyes widened, startled to see Obi out of her cage. Obi was just as startled to see Sweetie Smoochkins. For several moments, the two animals just stared at each other in shock and amazement.

Sweetie Smoochkins was the first to snap out of her daze. With a loud meow, she sprang toward Obi.

The little gerbil snapped out of *her* daze just as Sweetie Smoochkins was about to pounce. Obi darted into Rachel's bedroom. With Sweetie Smoochkins in hot pursuit, Obi sprinted across the carpet to Rachel's dresser.

Seeing that Obi was cornered, Sweetie Smoochkins slowed to a walk. "Now I've got you, Fuzzball!" she declared.

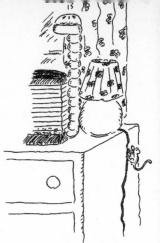

Obi, terrified, stopped. She was at the foot of Rachel's dresser. Tilting her head back, Obi gazed up at her cage on top of the dresser. How was she ever going to get back into her cage? She couldn't just leap up onto the top of the dresser the way the cat could.

Obi spied the electrical cord to the lamp that sat atop Rachel's dresser—the lamp cord that, earlier, she had slid down from. It was Obi's only hope. She raced over, clutched the cord in her small paws, and, like a human mountain climber, began to climb. Sweetie Smoochkins, who had never seen anything quite like this, just stared. She looked astounded. Within seconds, Obi had climbed to the top of Rachel's dresser. She hopped over Rachel's hairbrush and scrambled through the square opening of her cage door.

Sweetie Smoochkins suddenly came to her senses. The cat sprang up onto Rachel's dresser—just as Obi dropped down into the living room of her cage. But Obi was far from safe: her cage door was still hanging wide open. All Sweetie Smoochkins had to do was shove her paw through the square opening and—well, to skip all the messy details, let's just say that, for all you gerbil lovers, it would not have been a very pleasant sight. Luckily for Obi, the cat didn't seem to realize this. She was so used to sticking her paw through the bars of Obi's cage, it didn't occur to her that there might be another, easier, and far better and more efficient way to get at Obi.

From inside her cage, Obi frantically tried to swing her cage door shut. She couldn't get a good grip on the door, though. It was too far out. As Obi leaped out of the square opening, trying to grab the cage door with her little paws, Sweetie Smoochkins was less than five inches away, thrusting her big paw through the bars of Obi's living room. At one point, the two creatures glanced at each other. Their eyes met, locked. Obi saw a spark of intuition flicker in the cat's eyes. In that brief instant, Sweetie Smoochkins realized what she was doing wrong. Her face brightened. She pulled her paw out from the bars and sprang toward Obi.

With a terrified squeal, Obi leaped back into her cage. As she did so, the end of her tail got entangled in the bars of her cage door. As she flew back into her living room, Obi's tail, coiled in the bars, yanked the cage door shut—slamming it closed right in Sweetie Smoochkins's stunned face.

Obi landed on her living room floor in a heap of cedar shavings. She gasped for breath. Her whole body was trembling. Her heart felt like it was about to explode, it was thumping so furiously. Obi gazed at Sweetie Smoochkins on the other side of the bars.

Sweetie Smoochkins glared at Obi, her eyes blistering with rage. She swiped her paw through the air, hissed, and snarled, "I'll get you, Fuzzball! Just you wait!"

chapter Nineteen A Delicious Smell

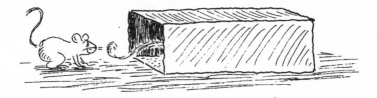

That night **obi lay** in her bedroom tower, wide-awake, unable to fall asleep. Her brain was buzzing. For one thing, she couldn't stop thinking about her big escape from her cage earlier that day. Freedom had felt so strange—and scary. And talk about scary, what a close call that was with Sweetie Smoochkins! Obi also couldn't stop thinking about Craig's two pets, Boa and José. She couldn't get over that (a) she had finally met them, and (b) that Craig would have such bizarre creatures for pets. As if all that wasn't enough, to add to Obi's insomnia, her stomach was making those loud, hungry, gurgling noises again.

Yet in one way, Obi was glad she couldn't fall asleep. She was terrified that she was going to have another dream about Mr. Armstrong.

As Obi lay there, she had the strange feeling again

that she was being secretly observed. Obi gazed about the darkened room, expecting to see one of the cats, but, like all the other times, she saw no one. She glanced over at Rachel's bedroom window, thinking it might be the squirrel peeking in at her. Nope, no squirrel. Was Obi just imagining it or was someone really watching her?

Yawning, Obi felt herself growing sleepy. She battled to stay awake. She did not want to have another nightmare. Really, truly, she didn't!

And then, all of a sudden, it was morning. The bedroom was filled with the soft, grayish light of dawn. Obi, waking, realized she had slept through the night. She had made it through the night without a nightmare about one of the cats or Craig's weird pets or even Mr. Armstrong.

"Whew, what a relief!" she sighed.

As Obi lay in her cedar shavings, she remembered the dream she had had about Mr. Armstrong the night before last. She remembered Mr. Armstrong's stern words: "You're a smart gerbil: you *can* figure it out. You just need to think about it."

Obi chuckled to herself at the very notion. "Oh, yeah, sure, *I* can figure it out. Hey, I'm just a little gerbil. I *can't* figure it out. I need someone to help me."

And then, just like that, Obi thought of someone.

If anyone could help Obi, it would be Mack, the old yellow Lab. He was a dog, after all, and dogs were extra special in the eyes of humans. How many books had Mr. Armstrong read to Rachel in which dogs saved the day? It had to be lots! Dogs were man's best friend! Surely, Mack would know of a way to let Tad know that Obi needed to be fed.

Obi wasted no time. She crawled down her tube to her living room. She stood on her hind legs and pushed open the cage door. She pulled herself up into the square opening, then hopped down onto the top of the dresser. She scrambled to the edge, where the lamp cord dropped over the side. Clutching the cord in her paws, Obi was about to descend when her gaze fell on her cage door.

It was wide-open.

If the cats were to visit, she realized, they would see the open cage door and then know that she had escaped. At which point, they were bound to come looking for her.

Obi dropped the cord and hurried back into her cage. She fluffed up the cedar shavings in her living room so that it would appear as if she was sleeping beneath a big mound of the wood flakes. Then she climbed back out of her cage, turned, and closed the little door. She shut it just enough so that, to the casual eye, it appeared closed. Then Obi dashed over to the edge of the dresser, grabbed the lamp cord in her paws, and slid down. She got to the floor, then scurried across the bedroom and out into the hallway.

Obi turned and headed in the direction of the stairs that went down to the first floor. She passed the upstairs bathroom. Then she came to the stairs that led up to the attic. As she was passing the attic stairs, she smelled something.

Something delicious!

She stopped and sniffed. It was a cheesy smell! It seemed to be coming from the attic. But how could that be? So far as Obi knew, the attic was where things that didn't get used very much or never got used at all anymore were kept.

Wow, I must be really hungry! thought Obi. I'm imagining I'm smelling cheese in the attic!

Obi continued on her way. She crept down the carpeted stairs to the first-floor hallway. Ever so quietly, she tiptoed over to the kitchen. Keeping out of sight, Obi peeked into the room. In the dim morning light, she saw the cats, all three of them, sleeping. Sugar

Smacks lay on the round kitchen table; Honey Buns was flopped on the cane seat of a kitchen chair; and Sweetie Smoochkins was sprawled out on the braided rug under the kitchen table. Obi stole past the doorway and continued down the dark hallway to the TV room.

All the pets in the TV room were asleep, too. Mack was on his comfy doggie bed in a deep slumber, with his eyes closed, snoring. Mr. Smithers was asleep in his cage that hung from the ceiling. Although Obi couldn't be sure, the goldfish, Betsy and Susie, seemed to be asleep, too, in their aquarium.

Obi stopped in front of Mack's face and tapped him gently on his moist, black nose.

"Psst, Mack," she whispered softly.

The old yellow Lab did not stir.

"Psst, Mack, wake up!" whispered Obi, her voice a little louder this time. "I need your help!"

Mack just let out a loud snore.

"Psst, Mack!" said Obi in an even louder whisper.

The old dog still did not wake.

Exasperated, Obi blurted out, "Oh, for goodness' sake, Mack! Wake up!"

To Obi's surprise, she heard a voice on the other side of the room—a loud, shrill cry from up in the air.

"Oh, for goodness' sake, Mack! Erp! Oh, for goodness' sake, Mack!"

Obi nearly jumped out of her fur, she was so startled. She whirled about and put her paw to her lips.

"Shh, Mr. Smithers!" she whispered.

In the shadowy light, she saw the parrot in his cage, perched on his small trapeze bar.

"Shh, Mr. Smithers! Shh, Mr. Smithers!" said the parrot.

Obi was terrified that Mr. Smithers was going to wake the cats. "Be quiet, Mr. Smithers!" she whispered. She waved her paws frantically in the air to try and get the parrot to hush up.

"Be quiet, Mr. Smithers! Erp! Be quiet, Mr. Smithers!"

Just then, out in the kitchen, Obi heard the patter of feet heading into the dining room. The kitchen was next to the dining room—which was across from the TV room.

Obi groaned. "That darn Mr. Smithers! He's woken up one of the cats!"

Obi had no choice but to hightail it out of the TV room, and fast. She dashed to the door that led out to the hallway, stuck her head out, saw no cats in sight, and took off.

A few moments later, Obi was hopping up the stairs on her way back to Rachel's bedroom. "That stupid, stupid, idiotic parrot!" she angrily muttered to herself. "What is his problem?"

Upon reaching the top of the stairs, Obi began to hurry down the hallway toward Rachel's bedroom. She was passing the stairs to the attic when, all of a sudden, she smelled it again: that wonderful, delicious, cheesy smell! What kind of cheese was it? Obi stopped and sniffed the air. It wasn't Swiss cheese, nor a Camembert. Not Muenster, either. It smelled more like . . . oh, my gosh, it was Obi's absolute favorite kind of cheese: Cheddar!

Obi closed her eyes and breathed in the luscious cheesy aroma. Gosh, it smelled so good! It also reminded Obi of how ravenously hungry she was.

And then, as if in a trance, Obi's eyes glazed over. She turned and began to hop up the stairs that led up to the attic. The cheesy aroma had a magical, hypnotic spell on Obi, luring her forward. When she got to the top step, Obi dropped to her stomach and squeezed under the attic door.

The attic was dark, much darker than the rest of the house. It also smelled terribly musty. So musty, in fact, that, for a moment, Obi lost the scent of the cheese. She paused, waiting for her eyes to adjust to the dark. When they did, Obi glanced about the attic, searching for that piece of scrumptious Cheddar cheese. It was amazing to see all the stuff that the Armstrongs kept up here. There were boxes and boxes of old books, plus boxes of old magazines and boxes of old record albums. There were shoes lying about. A baby crib. Old sleds. Skis and ski helmets and boots and poles. Clothes. Framed prints and posters. Board games like Monopoly, Mouse Trap, Scrabble, and Clue. Obi ventured forward, her eyes darting about the attic, searching for that piece of fragrant cheese.

The scent seemed to be coming from the far end of the attic, near the triangular-shaped wall with a small window whose panes of glass were filthy with dust. Obi hurried in that direction, sniffing. As she approached the wall, she spied a small rectangular box lying on the dusty floorboards. The box was about the same size and shape as a box of animal crackers. It was open at each end. No doubt about it, the cheesy smell was drifting out from inside this box. Obi stopped and took another deep whiff of the delightful aroma. Her eyes softened in a dreamy sort of way. She lifted her left front paw to step into the box.

"Ah, cheese, here I come," she murmured.

And then suddenly, from out of the shadows, something darted out and tackled her.

Obi's first thought was that it was one of the cats. But the creature was much too small to be a cat. (Not to mention, why would a cat be in the attic?) The creature struck Obi so unexpectedly and with such force that the two of them went tumbling across the dusty floorboards, smacking into an old, retired toaster. Obi, blinking, found herself on her back, staring up into the face of a small, scraggly, elderly mouse.

chapter Twenty Mr. Durkins

The old mouse was so close to Obi, his face was practically touching hers. He was a very old mouse, with grizzled whiskers, white fur on his snout, and a fierce, intense look in his tiny, beady eyes. Obi, terrified, let out a shriek. "Get off me, you creep!" she cried, and pushed the old mouse off her.

"Creep?" said the old mouse, sounding surprised, as he hopped to his feet. "Who you calling a creep?"

"You, that's who!" said Obi. She sprang to her feet, brushing the dust off her fur. "How dare you tackle me like that!"

"How dare you talk to me like that!" said the old mouse, all in a huff. "I just saved your life, kid."

"What are you talking about?" said Obi.

"You know that box you were about to step into?" said the old mouse.

"Yeah? What about it?"

"It's a trap!"

"A trap?" said Obi. "That's how much you know. It's got my absolute favorite cheese inside it—Cheddar cheese!"

"Cheddar cheese, my whiskers!" said the old mouse. "There's no cheese in that box. You were about to step into a trap, kid. A death trap!"

Obi was stunned. She stared in horror at the old mouse. "A *death trap*?"

The old mouse nodded. "The floor of that box is covered with sticky glue. If you had stepped into that box, you never would've stepped out."

Shocked, Obi stared at the box. She placed her paw over her heart and cried, "Who—who put *that* in the Armstrongs' attic?"

"Mr. Armstrong, that's *who*!"

"Rachel's *father*?" cried Obi, staring in disbelief at the old mouse. "You don't know what you're talking about!"

"Oh, no?" said the old mouse. "Then how come I saw him put it there with my own two eyes?"

"Maybe it was someone else."

"He's tall. Wears glasses. Kind of a funny nose. Always looks like he needs a haircut."

That was Mr. Armstrong, all right. Obi felt so confused. Why would Mr. Armstrong do such a thing? How could he be so cruel? Obi suddenly felt faint, almost dizzy. She leaned back on the side of the old toaster to steady herself.

"Hey, you okay?" asked the old mouse, eyeing Obi with a look of concern.

"I—I feel a little faint," confessed Obi.

"Well, considering you haven't eaten in days, that's not surprising."

Obi stared at the old mouse. "How did you know that?"

"Look how skinny you are," said the old mouse. "It's obvious you haven't been eating."

Obi nodded. "Well, it's true. I haven't had any food in days. Nor water. I'll be okay in a minute."

"Here, lean on me."

As the old mouse came to Obi, she noticed he walked with a limp. The old mouse helped Obi over to a plastic orange cup that was lying on its side. It was a human toddler's tippy cup that was missing its top. Evidently, the cup must have fallen out of one of the boxes in the attic. The old mouse turned the cup upside down so Obi could sit on it. "Stay here," he ordered. "I'll be right back."

"Where are you going?"

"Just stay here."

As Obi watched, the old mouse limped over to a bunch of brown boxes that said FRAGILE in red letters along their sides. He disappeared down a narrow alleyway between two of the boxes. Alone, Obi glanced about the dark, cluttered attic. Her gaze fell upon the small, rectangular, open-ended box—that dangerous, evil death trap—that sat on the floor not far away, beckoning with its cheesy aroma. Obi shuddered to think how close she had come to stepping inside it—and to her own death! And to think Rachel's own father would have been the cause!

To take her mind off death traps and horrible death, Obi turned and peered in the other direction. Her eyes focused on the old toaster; she saw her reflection in the shiny metal side of the appliance. She gasped at the

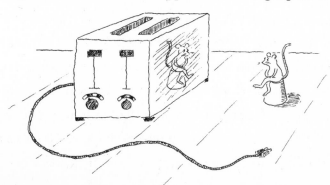

sight of herself. "Oh, my gosh! Look how scrawny I've become!"

In all likelihood, Obi, at this point, would have gotten all stressed out and wrung her paws in despair at how perfectly dreadful she looked. But just at that moment, she heard a noise up by the small square window behind her. It was a loud, scratchy sort of noise. Obi turned and, peering up at the window, spotted a twitching tail of gray, feathery fur. No doubt who that was; it was that nutcase, the gray squirrel. He was on the uppermost part of the Armstrongs' roof, apparently looking for acorns. The squirrel's head abruptly popped up in one of the dirty windowpanes. He had an acorn stuffed in his mouth. He started to turn to go when his eye caught sight of Obi in the attic. Startled, the squirrel did a double take. He looked terrified. His eyeballs bulged, his jaw dropped open, and the acorn dropped out of his mouth. Why did he look so frightened? Obi wondered. It's just *me*. And then Obi remembered the conversation she had had with the squirrel the day before, and how he thought she was in jail.

Oh, no! thought Obi. That goofy squirrel thinks I've busted out of my cage. He must think I'm an escaped convict!

Obi heard a shuffling sound over by the stack of boxes. It was the old mouse, emerging from the shadowy alleyway. Obi saw the squirrel's gaze shift from her to the old mouse. The squirrel's eyes grew even larger and more terrified. He abruptly whirled about and leaped from the window, vanishing from view.

Obi couldn't figure out why the squirrel was so scared to see a little old mouse. Then it dawned on her that if the squirrel thought she was an escaped convict, he must think the old mouse was part of her criminal gang. He probably thought he'd stumbled upon their secret hideout!

The old mouse had not seen the squirrel. He hobbled toward Obi, carrying something in his mouth. It was a big, brownish-white clump of—well, Obi wasn't quite sure what it was.

When the old mouse got to Obi, he stopped, took the clump out of his mouth, broke off a small piece, and held it out to Obi. "Here, eat this," he said.

"What is it?" asked Obi.

"Bread."

"Bread!" cried Obi excitedly. She grabbed the small piece out of the old mouse's paws and bit into it. She nearly broke a tooth. The bread was as hard as a rock.

"Sorry, it's a little stale," said the old mouse.

"Who cares?" cried Obi, chewing. "At least it's food! Thank you so much!"

"Wow, you really are hungry!" said the old mouse as he watched Obi gobble down the rest of the small piece of bread. Instead of giving Obi another small piece, the old mouse just handed her the entire scrap of bread, crust and all. "Sorry it's not Cheddar cheese," he said. "That's my absolute favorite cheese, too."

"Cheddar cheese would be nice, but this bread is just what I need at the moment," said Obi. "It tastes so good!" As Obi noisily chomped on the stale bread, she peered at the old mouse and said, "So who are you anyway?"

"The name is Malcolm Durkins."

"What are you doing in the Armstrongs' attic, Mr. Durkins?"

"This is my home," replied the old mouse.

"You mean the Armstrongs' home, don't you?" said Obi.

"No, *my* home," said the old mouse gruffly. "I was here long before the Armstrongs ever moved in."

"You were?"

The old mouse nodded. "Used to be a thriving colony of mice that lived in this house."

"What happened to them?"

"They got killed off," said the old mouse. "Well, all but me."

"That's terrible!" exclaimed Obi. "Who killed them?"

"The Armstrongs!" said the old mouse bitterly.

"The Armstrongs?" said Obi, aghast. "Not Rachel! She would never do such a thing!"

"Well, no, not her, but her father and her mother would, did."

"*Mrs.* Armstrong?" said Obi incredulously. She was having enough trouble accepting the fact that Mr. Armstrong would do such a horrible thing as set out a death trap. But Mrs. Armstrong, too?

"You know those three cats?" said the old mouse.

"You mean Sugar Smacks, Honey Buns, and Sweetie Smoochkins?"

"Yeah, them," said the old mouse, his voice dripping with scorn. "You know why Mrs. Armstrong got them?"

Obi shook her head.

"To get rid of the mice."

"Really!" said Obi. "I've always wondered why she got those cats."

"That's why," said the old mouse. He heaved a deep, sad sigh. "Now I'm the only one left."

"I'm sorry," said Obi. She reached out and gently put her paw on the old mouse's shoulder to comfort him.

A dramatic change came over the old mouse. His face hardened, his beady little eyes narrowed to slits. "Don't worry," he said. "I'm getting my revenge. Now I torment them!"

"Torment who?" asked Obi, startled by this abrupt change in the old mouse's demeanor. He sounded bitter. Very bitter. She removed her paw from the old mouse's shoulder.

"The Armstrongs!" said the old mouse. "I drive them crazy! Especially *Mr.* Armstrong!"

"How do you do that?" asked Obi. She didn't like the way the old mouse had begun to talk. He spoke with such vengeance, such hate. It really frightened Obi.

"I lurk in the shadows and then scurry out so they see me just for a split second out of the corner of their eyes. But when they turn to take a closer look, I'm gone!" The old mouse, looking rather gleeful, rubbed his front paws together and let out a fiendish chuckle. "It drives them nuts! They don't know if I exist or not! That's why Mr. Armstrong put out that death trap. He's hoping to catch me. But he never will. I'm much too smart for him."

Obi did not like the direction the conversation had taken. She decided it was time to change the subject. "Well, this has been a delicious meal," she said. "I can't tell you how hungr—"

The old mouse suddenly held up his paw. "Shh! Listen!"

Obi stopped chewing and listened. She didn't hear anything, though. "What is it?" she asked.

"I heard a dog bark downstairs. Music Boy must be here."

"Music Boy?" said Obi, puzzled.

"That kid with the earphones."

"Oh, you mean Tad!" said Obi. She laughed at the thought of the old mouse calling him "Music Boy." Obi made an attempt at a joke. "He wears those earphones so much, it's amazing they don't get stuck in his ears."

The old mouse did not chuckle, though. Didn't even smile or look amused. "Hear that?" he said. "Now the cats are meowing."

"The cats always meow when Tad—I mean, Music Boy—arrives," said Obi.

The old mouse got to his feet and said, "Come on!"

"Where are we going?" asked Obi, who, to be perfectly honest, would have preferred to sit and eat a bit more of the stale bread.

"Follow me!" ordered the old mouse as, limping, he hurried behind a pair of old black ski boots that sat near one of the two sloping walls that gave the attic ceiling its upside-down V shape.

chapter Twenty-one

The Secret
Passageway

"**W**hat's back here?" asked Obi as she hurried to keep up with Mr. Durkins. For an old mouse with a limp, he certainly moved fast! It was so dark behind the ski equipment and all the big cardboard boxes, it was hard to see. Obi stopped. The old mouse had vanished.

"Mr. Durkins?" asked Obi as she glanced about the shadowy darkness.

"In here!"

Strangely, it sounded like the old mouse's voice had come from within the wall. Straining her eyes, Obi noticed a small black smudge upon the dark wall by the floorboards. Looking closer, Obi saw that the smudge was a little hole. "Are you in the wall, Mr. Durkins?"

"Yes, now get in here!"

Obi wasn't sure if she should enter or not. More than

once, she had heard both Mr. and Mrs. Armstrong tell Rachel that she should always, always be careful around strangers. She should never, for instance, get into a stranger's human mobile. Mr. Durkins was a stranger. But he also had saved Obi's life. And fed her. It seemed to Obi that if he was going to try any funny business, he probably would have tried it by now. More to the point, Mr. Durkins had a limp, was rather elderly, and, being a mouse, was smaller than Obi. She was reasonably sure that if Mr. Durkins misbehaved or tried to harm her, she would be able to handle herself. Still, she would be on her guard at all times.

"What's in here?" asked Obi as she cautiously stepped through the hole. In the darkness, she spotted the small, hunched-over form of Mr. Durkins. He was waiting for her under one of the splintery timbers that supported the Armstrongs' roof.

"It's a secret passageway," replied Mr. Durkins. The old mouse turned and, limping, began to lead the way through the dark passageway.

"This is so cool!" cried Obi. "A secret passageway in the Armstrongs' house! Who knew?"

"Nobody knows about it but me," said the old mouse.

And now me, thought Obi. "Where does it lead to?" she asked.

"It goes all over the house."

"Cool!"

"Cool?" said the old mouse. "You sound like a human." He said it in a very nasty, contemptuous tone of voice. Clearly, he did not think much of one of Rachel's favorite expressions.

"Oh, sorry," apologized Obi. She made a mental note to herself not to use the word "cool" again in front of the old mouse. "I have a tube. You know, a tunnel," said Obi as she followed the old mouse past a strip of drooping fiberglass insulation that sagged from the ceiling. "But it's not like this! Not at all! *This* is amazing! Hey, what are these drawings on the walls?" She had noticed some primitive, stick-figure drawings on the old timbers that they were hurrying past. The drawings, which looked as if they had been made with crayons, were of mice and humans. The mice were shown running away from the humans, who were armed with brooms and looked like ugly monsters.

"Those were made long ago by my ancestors," said the old mouse.

"Gosh, they look like cave paintings!"

"Cave paintings?" said the old mouse, peering quizzically at Obi over his shoulder.

"Oh, Mr. Armstrong once read a book about them to Rachel," explained Obi. "Since my cage is in Rachel's bedroom, I get to listen."

The old mouse abruptly stopped and whirled about. "Listen, kid," he said. "Let's get one thing straight. You're a rodent, not a human."

"I know I am," said Obi.

"You don't sound like you know."

"Well, I do," insisted Obi. "I know I'm a gerbil. Honest!"

"Okay, keep your voice down," said the old mouse as they continued on their way through the dark tunnel, which had begun to slope downward. "We're almost there."

"Almost where?"

"The kitchen."

Obi gasped. She was horrified. "We're—we're going into the kitchen? But that's where—that's where the cats are!"

"Hey, keep your voice down, will ya!" whispered the old mouse sternly. "We're not going *into* the kitchen. We're just going to observe."

"Observe?" whispered Obi, puzzled. "From where?"

"From here," said the old mouse. He stopped in front of a little hole in the wall. It was a tiny hole—just big enough, really, for a small mouse to crawl through. "There they are!" the old mouse whispered, peering through the hole, his face lit by the light from the kitchen.

Obi crammed her head into the hole, too, and peeked out. Sure enough, there were Sugar Smacks, Honey Buns, and Sweetie Smooch-kins. The three cats were by the big  white plastic garbage can, with their backs to them. Each cat was eating from a small bowl. Evidently, Tad had just fed them. As Sugar Smacks was munching on her dry cat food, she turned her head and peered in the direction of the hole—as if she knew she was being observed! Obi quickly ducked her head out of sight.

"Don't worry," whispered the old mouse. "The cats have no idea we're here. They're so clueless."

"Where are we?" asked Obi. "I mean, I know we're in the kitchen, but where?"

"By the stove," replied the old mouse.

"Wow, this is so—" Obi was about to say "cool" again, but she caught herself just in time. "Neat."

"I wonder where Music Boy is?" muttered the old mouse. Then, to Obi, he said, "Come on!"

Limping, Mr. Durkins hurried through the secret passageway, with Obi right behind him. They came to another little opening. The old mouse and Obi peeked out of the hole. They were now in the TV room. Obi saw Mack, Mr. Smithers, and Betsy and Susie, the goldfish. Evidently, Tad had already been here, too, for all the pets were eating. Mack sat on his bed, chomping on a dog biscuit; Mr. Smithers was in his cage, nibbling on a suet cake; and the goldfish were darting about in their aquarium, gobbling up the flakes of fish food that floated on the surface of the water.

"Not here, either," said the old mouse. "He must be up in Craig's bedroom."

Obi, horrified, stared at the old mouse. "We're not going *there*, are we? Craig has two dangerous pets, you know: a snake and a tarantula!"

The old mouse scoffed. "Those losers! They don't scare me!"

Mr. Durkins swung about and headed back through the passageway in the direction that they had come. At one point, the passageway split into two directions. The old mouse scurried into the passageway that sloped upward.

"Where's this other tunnel go?" Obi asked.

"To the downstairs hallway," replied the old mouse. "It comes out behind the old grandfather clock."

"Really?!" said Obi in surprise. She had rolled past the old grandfather clock in her Gerbil Mobile a zillion times. Not once had it ever occurred to her that a little mouse hole might be nearby.

"C'mon, move faster," said Mr. Durkins impatiently. "You run faster on your exercise wheel."

"How do you know about my exercise wheel?" asked Obi as she hurried to keep up with Mr. Durkins. The old mouse was in such a hurry, though, he didn't respond.

The secret passageway brought them back upstairs, and then it split in two again. Mr. Durkins took the passageway that led off to the right. They passed another little peephole.

"This looks out to the upstairs hallway," said the old mouse.

"What about this hole?" asked Obi as they approached another hole farther down the passageway. She stopped and peeked out of the small opening. To her total astonishment, she found herself gazing into Rachel's bedroom. It was a spectacular view from somewhere near the bedroom closet.

"Hey, I know this room!" said Obi.

"C'mon!" said the old mouse, sounding even more impatient, if such a thing was possible. "Stop dawdling!"

As Obi pulled her head from the hole, she realized something. She was surprised she hadn't figured it out sooner. "*You're* the one who's been spying on me, aren't you?"

The old mouse did not respond. He just continued hobbling down the shadowy passageway.

"It is *you*, isn't it?"

"I watch everyone," grumbled the old mouse. "Nothing happens in this house without my knowledge."

"I *knew* I was being watched!" said Obi as she caught up with the old mouse. They came to another little hole. The old mouse and Obi stuck their heads into the hole and gazed out. They were looking out into Craig's darkened bedroom.

"Well, we found Music Boy," said the old mouse.

They sure had. The teenage boy was standing by Craig's desk. On the desk sat two aquariums, one large, one small. The large aquarium was the snake's home; the smaller one belonged to the tarantula. Tad had taken Boa, the corn snake, out of his aquarium and was playing with him. He had the snake wrapped around his neck. The snake's face was just inches from Tad's face.

"Eeeewwww!" cried Obi, shuddering. "How disgusting!" Obi put her paws over her eyes so she wouldn't have to see. But only for a second. Disgusting as the sight was, it was still pretty amazing to be able to see this without anyone knowing you were there.

"This secret passageway is so cool, Mr. Durkins!" whispered Obi. The moment she said it, she realized her mistake: she had used the "cool" word again. She pulled her head out of the hole and placed both front paws over her mouth.

The old mouse visibly cringed. He didn't say anything, though. He continued to watch Tad for a bit longer, and then he, too, pulled his head from the hole. "Let's go back to the attic," he said. "It's time for your indoctrination."

"My what?" asked Obi.

"Your indoctrination," said the old mouse as they made their way through the passageway back to the attic.

"What on earth is *that*?" It was not a word Obi was familiar with. It certainly wasn't a word she remembered Mr. Armstrong uttering when he read aloud children's books to Rachel.

"Your school lesson," replied the old mouse.

"I'm going to *school*?" asked Obi, surprised and frowning. "Why am I going to school? What am I going to learn? How long do I have to go to school for?"

The old mouse turned and gave Obi a sharp glance. "Anyone ever tell you that you're a chatterbox?"

"No," said Obi.

"Well, you are!" snapped the old mouse. "Now button it up, will you, till we get back to the attic."

Obi was offended and, frankly, rather hurt that the old mouse would talk to her in such a gruff manner. A chatterbox?! Obi decided she would not say another word to Mr. Durkins, the old curmudgeon. And she didn't! Even when they got back to the attic, Obi refused to speak. Mr. Durkins disappeared into the shadows behind an ancient upright vacuum cleaner. A few moments later, he reappeared, limping into view with what appeared to be—wow, could it be?!—a round chocolate sandwich cookie with white creamy filling! When Obi saw this, there was no way she could possibly keep quiet.

"Is that a *cookie*? Where did you get *that*?"

"From Music Boy," replied the old mouse in a very matter-of-fact tone of voice.

"Tad gave *you* a cookie?" Obi asked, surprised.

"No, of course not!" said Mr. Durkins. He stopped in front of Obi and broke off a small piece of the cookie. "The other day Music Boy dropped some cookies in the upstairs hallway."

"Hey, I saw him drop those cookies!" cried Obi. "It happened right in front of Rachel's bedroom doorway."

The old mouse snickered. "Know why Music Boy dropped them?"

Obi shook her head. "No, why?"

"Because Yours Truly ran out and startled him. The moment the cookies fell onto the carpet, I grabbed one, then dashed back into the secret passageway."

"Well, that explains that!" said Obi.

"Now, here's what we're going to do," said the old mouse. "I'm going to teach you your school lessons. Every time you get something right, you'll be rewarded with a little piece of the cookie. Okay?"

"Okay," said Obi.

The old mouse was about to begin the lesson when Obi raised her paw.

"Yes?" he said.

"How come you didn't give me the cookie before?" asked Obi. "You know, instead of that piece of stale bread."

"I needed the cookie as an incentive," replied the old mouse. "Now, lesson number one."

Obi raised her paw again.

Looking a little exasperated, Mr. Durkins said, "What is it?"

"What's an incentive?"

"It's something exciting," responded the old mouse. "Something that causes you to work really hard because you want it so badly."

"I see," said Obi, nodding.

"Now, lesson number—"

Obi lifted her paw again.

"What is it *this time*?" demanded the old mouse, losing his patience.

"Why do you need an incentive?"

"To make sure you'll learn your lessons," he replied. "I knew a cookie was something special that you'd really want." Before he could be interrupted again, the old mouse quickly continued, "Now, lesson number one! Repeat after me: I hate the Armstrongs!"

Obi, blinking, gaped at the old mouse. This was not exactly what she thought her school lesson was going to be about. "But I don't hate the Armstrongs!" she said.

"Then you don't get any cookie," said Mr. Durkins.

Obi's eyes fell on the cookie. It looked so delicious. Particularly that white creamy filling. Obi suddenly felt ravenously hungry. "But I'm starving, Mr. Durkins!" said Obi. "I need to eat!"

"Well, if you learn your lesson, you'll eat," said the old mouse. "It's as simple as that, kid. You need to understand the relationship between humans and rodents. They hate us and we hate them. So repeat after me: I hate the Armstrongs."

Obi did not want to say this. But she was feeling weak from hunger again. Obi tried to reason with herself. What would be the harm of saying it? It wasn't as if she actually had to *mean* it.

"I . . . I hate the Armstrongs," said Obi.

"Good!" cried the old mouse, grinning. He handed Obi a little piece of the cookie.

Obi popped it into her mouth. It tasted scrumptious.

"Lesson number two," said the old mouse. "I hate Mr. Armstrong!"

Obi did not want to say this, either. Once again, though, she told herself she could say it without really meaning it. "I . . . I hate Mr. Armstrong."

Obi was expecting another piece of cookie, but the old mouse did not give her one. "Next," he said. "I hate Mrs. Armstrong!"

To help her say this, Obi thought of all those times that Mrs. Armstrong had flicked on Rachel's bedroom ceiling light at six-thirty on dark, cold winter mornings, waking Rachel—and Obi—up. "I hate Mrs. Armstrong."

"Very good!" said the old mouse. He handed Obi another small piece of cookie.

"Lesson three: I hate Craig!"

This one was easy to say. "I hate Craig!" said Obi.

"I hate the twins!" said the old mouse.

"I hate the twins!" said Obi. To Obi's surprise, it was becoming easier and easier to use the "hate" word.

"We're making excellent progress!" said the old mouse, looking quite pleased. His dark, beady eyes shone brightly.

"Now for the final lesson of the day. I hate Rachel!"

No, not Rachel! thought Obi. That was going too far! Much too far! There was no way Obi could—or would—say such a thing. Even if she didn't mean it, she could never say she hated her adopted mother! "I'm sorry, Mr. Durkins, but I can't say that."

"You must!" cried the old mouse fiercely.

"I can't!" protested Obi. "Please don't make me say it!"

"All right!" said the old mouse. "Don't say it. But no more cookie! It's your choice!"

Obi heard her stomach growl. She felt so hungry. It was as if the piece of stale bread and the little pieces of cookie that she had wolfed down had awakened her stomach and reminded Obi of just how famished she was. Just say it, Obi, she told herself. You don't have to mean it.

"I . . . I . . . I . . . I . . ." stammered Obi in a voice that was not much louder than a whisper.

"Go on, say it!" ordered the old mouse.

"I . . . I hate . . ."

But try as she might, Obi could not finish the statement. She was nearly in tears.

"Go on, you're almost there!" coached the old mouse. "Just say it and I'll give you this big piece of cookie."

The old mouse broke off a large chunk of the cookie and held it in front of Obi's nose.

"You've almost said it, kid," said Mr. Durkins. "C'mon, you can do it! I know you can!"

With tears in her eyes, Obi tried again. "I . . . I hate . . . I hate . . . I hate Ra—"

The old mouse waved the big piece of cookie back and forth in front of Obi's face. "Go on! Say it!" he said.

"I . . . I hate . . . I hate Ra . . . Ra . . . Rach—No! No! No! No! *NOOOO*!" cried Obi, stamping her foot on the floor. "I don't hate Rachel!" Obi grabbed the big piece of cookie out of the old mouse's paw and violently flung it at the old mouse. "Here, take your darn old cookie, you

wicked old mouse! I don't hate Rachel! I love Rachel and she loves me!"

Obi swung around and marched toward the attic door to head back to her cage.

"Hey, kid," the old mouse called out after her. "Let me ask you something. If Rachel loves you so much, how come Music Boy isn't feeding you while she's away?"

Obi stopped, turned, and glared at the old mouse. "I don't know why," she said. "But I still know she loves me!"

"Oh, I think you know why," said the old mouse. "Rachel forgot you! Seems to me if she really loved you she wouldn't have forgotten you."

"You're wrong!" cried Obi. "Rachel does love me and she would never forget me!"

"There's one way to find out," said the old mouse.

"How?" asked Obi. She lifted her paw to her face and wiped the tears from her eyes.

"The Armstrongs left Music Boy instructions on feeding the pets," said Mr. Durkins. "The sheet of paper is on the kitchen table. If you're mentioned in the instructions, well, then I guess that would prove she does love you."

Obi could not believe the old mouse. He actually wanted her to go into the *kitchen*? He wasn't serious, was he? The cats hung out in the kitchen. The cats would attack poor Obi the moment they set eyes on her. There was no way they'd ever let her get near the kitchen table, let alone near the instructions on top of the table. "But I can't—" Obi started to say when the old mouse interrupted.

"Don't tell me you can't read, kid, because I know you can. I've watched you when Mr. Armstrong is reading to Rachel. I've seen your lips move."

Obi was startled that the old mouse knew her secret. "I was going to say I can't go into the kitchen. That's where the cats hang out. They'd never let me get near the kitchen table."

"If you really want to find out if Rachel loves you, you'll find a way," replied the old mouse.

"Good-bye, Mr. Durkins," said Obi. "Thank you for feeding me and thank you for saving my life from that horrible death trap. I'm sorry to have to say this, but I hope I never see you again."

"Go take a look at that sheet of paper," said the old mouse. "Find out the truth, Obi."

It was the first time the old mouse had called Obi by her name. Under different circumstances, Obi might have felt elated, even touched, that the old mouse had actually spoken her name instead of calling her "kid." But not now. Now she turned and walked across the dusty old floorboards toward the light shining underneath the attic door.

By **the time** Obi slipped back into her cage, she was sobbing. She felt so terribly confused and just plain miserable. She knew whom she hated, and it was not Rachel. She hated that wretched old Mr. Durkins. Why did he have to say those horrible things about Obi's adopted mother? Obi knew she should feel grateful to the old mouse for saving her life, but why did he have to put those ugly thoughts into her head? Couldn't he just have saved Obi and left it at that?

That night, like every night since Rachel and her family had been gone, Obi had the worst time falling asleep. Tonight, though, it was not an empty stomach that kept her awake. Or the thought of having a nightmare. No, this time it was her heart. It felt as if it was being twisted and yanked in all different directions. Obi had so many questions. Why wasn't Tad feeding her? Had Rachel really forgotten her? Had her adopted mother actually forgotten to leave instructions for Tad to feed her? Obi hated to admit it, but it was just like Rachel to forget something important like that. But just because Rachel might have forgotten, it didn't mean she didn't love Obi. Did it? No, of course not! It simply meant she was a forgetful kid. But if she had forgotten to leave instructions for Tad, wouldn't Rachel remember Obi while she was on vacation? Wouldn't she call Tad on the phone and beg him to feed Obi?

"Please, Tad, I forgot to tell you before I left to feed Obi! Quick, Tad, get over to my house right away and go feed Obi! The poor little thing is starving!"

Yes, she would absolutely do that! Unless, that is, the old mouse was right and Rachel really didn't love her and had forgotten all about her little gerbil. A lump formed in Obi's throat and her eyes welled up with tears as she thought this. Then Obi thought: What am I saying? Of course Rachel loves me and would never forget me! It's all Tad's fault. It's got to be! He's so busy listening to music on those gosh-darn earphones, he probably hasn't even looked closely at the instructions that are sitting right on the kitchen table!

Obi sighed. As much as she hated to admit it, she

knew the old mouse was right: there was only one way to find out the truth. She would have to read those instructions. But to do that, she would have to sneak into the kitchen, get past the cats, and climb up onto the kitchen table. How would she ever accomplish *that*?

Obi got busy devising a plan. At first she had trouble thinking of what to do. But then she remembered what always happened whenever she ventured downstairs and, just like that, the plan came to her. Rather than put her plan into effect right that minute, though, she decided to get some sleep. Her plan was a dangerous one (at least for a gerbil), and she wanted to be good and alert when she carried it out.

Early the next morning, in the gray smudgy light of dawn, Obi quietly snuck out of her cage. Like the day before, she patted together a mound of cedar shavings so the cats, if they happened to drop by, would think she was asleep beneath the pile. Then she shut her cage door so it would appear that it was tightly closed. Out in the hallway, Obi turned in the direction that led downstairs.

The first thing Obi did when she arrived downstairs was to check on the cats. So far so good: all three were in the kitchen, asleep in their usual spots on and around the kitchen table. Obi continued down the hallway to the TV room. Mack lay sprawled on his doggie bed, deep in slumber and snoring loudly—no surprise there. The goldfish were also asleep in their underwater castle. Mr. Smithers was asleep, too, in his cage. His eyes were shut and his beak was resting upon his feathered chest.

"Psst, Mr. Smithers," whispered Obi, standing beneath the parrot's cage. "Wake up!"

No response.

"Mr. Smithers!" whispered Obi again, a little louder this time.

The parrot, stirring, opened an eye.

"It's me, Obi," whispered Obi. She waved a paw at him.

Looking startled, the parrot opened both eyes wide and jerked his head up. "Erp!" he said.

"Hawo!" whispered Obi.

"Hawo! Hawo!" echoed Mr. Smithers.

"Shh!" said Obi. "I need your help."

"Help! Help!" cried the parrot.

Obi, flustered, frantically waved her

front paws at Mr. Smithers to hush up. "Shh, quiet, Mr. Smithers!"

"Shh, quiet, Mr. Smithers!" repeated the parrot.

"Oh, for goodness' sake!" muttered Obi, annoyed and exasperated. Couldn't Mr. Smithers do anything right? Obi decided to get right to her plan. She crept over to the doorway that led into the hallway. "Obi is loose!" she called out. "Obi is loose!"

"Erp, Obi is loose! Obi is loose!" echoed the parrot.

"Gerbil on the loose! Gerbil on the loose!" Obi cried out again.

"Gerbil on the loose! Erp! Gerbil on the loose!" repeated the parrot.

By now, Obi was so nervous, her heart felt like it was going to pound right out of her chest.

"Gerbil on the loose! Gerbil on the loose!" cried the parrot.

"In the dining room! In the dining room!" cried Obi.

"In the dining room! In the dining room!" screeched the parrot.

Obi heard a cat jump down onto the floor of the kitchen. Then she heard two other cats spring onto the floor. Then she heard the patter of cat feet hurrying into the dining room.

Mr. Smithers, meanwhile, was acting like a smoke detector that had gone off and wouldn't shut up. "Gerbil on the loose! Gerbil on the loose! In the dining room! In the dining room!"

Obi realized that it was time for her to make her next move. Taking a deep breath, she dashed down the hallway. When she got to the kitchen doorway, she stopped and peered in. Not a cat in sight. Okay, thought Obi. Here I go!

Obi fixed her gaze on the kitchen table and scurried across the tiled floor. When she was nearly at the table, she took a flying leap into the air straight toward one of the kitchen chairs. Perfect! She landed right on the cane seat. Obi stood on her hind legs and, with her front paws, grabbed hold of the linen tablecloth. She dug her claws into the fabric and hoisted herself up onto the top of the table.

It felt so weird to be on the table where Rachel and her family ate their meals. But Obi had no time to think about this. She glanced about the table for the sheet of paper with Tad's instructions. She didn't see it, though. The only thing she saw was a stack of music CDs. Obi recognized the top CD. It was Rachel's CD! Then Obi saw the titles that were on the sides of the other CD cases. It was all Rachel's music. Obi frowned. How weird! What were Rachel's CDs doing on the kitchen table? Then Obi remembered the wicked, horrid plan that Tad and Craig had schemed up back on that morning that the Armstrongs left for vacation. To save Craig from having to listen to Rachel's CDs during the trip, Tad had hidden her CDs in the cabinet above the stove so Mr. Armstrong wouldn't see them and pack them in the human mobile. The plan had called for Tad to take the CDs out from the cabinet after the Armstrongs left and place them on the kitchen table so it would appear, when the Armstrongs returned from vacation, as if Mr. Armstrong had forgotten to pack them. From the looks of things, everything so far had gone according to the two boys' evil plan.

Obi wandered around the stack of CDs. As she did so, she spotted it—the instructions! A salt and a pepper shaker sat on top of the sheet of notebook paper. Obi stepped onto the paper and began to read.

Tad, please be sure to give Mack one can of dog food and one scoop of dry dog food in the morning and evening. You'll find both in the pantry in the kitchen. He also needs to be let outside for a few minutes. The cats' food is also in the pantry. They each get dry cat food in the morning and a can of cat food in the evening. Their litter box is in the basement. You should change it at the end of the week. Mr. Smithers should be fed once a day. His food is in the TV room, as is the fish food. The goldfish get fed twice, once in the morning and once in the evening. They get just a sprinkle. If you need to reach us, we're at

Several phone numbers with area codes were listed at the bottom of the paper.

Obi, blinking, stared at the note. That was it—that was the end of the instructions. Not a single word about feeding Obi!

Nothing at all!

Obi felt her eyes growing wet with tears. But then Obi thought of something. Maybe her name was hidden under the salt or pepper shaker.

She turned and, with her rear end, pushed the salt shaker off the piece of paper. Then she pushed the pepper shaker off. Then she turned to take another look at the instructions.

Alas, nothing more had been written under either the salt or pepper shaker.

So the old mouse was right. Rachel had forgotten

Obi. A tear slipped from Obi's eye and plopped down onto the sheet of notebook paper. The drop landed on one of the words that were written in blue pen. The ink instantly swelled and blurred, turning the teardrop blue.

"Well, well, well! Look who we have here!" an all-too-familiar voice said from behind Obi.

Being the skittish creature she was, Obi should have been startled out of her wits. She should have leaped off the table and tried to scamper away. But Obi didn't. Instead, she just let out a sigh—a deep, despairing sigh—turned and, in a weepy voice, said, "Hawo, Sugar Smacks."

As Obi gazed into Sugar Smacks's large, gleaming eyes, she was surprised she didn't feel more concerned for her life. After all, Sugar Smacks was only a few inches away. No bars, no layer of thick Gerbil Mobile plastic separated Obi from the cat. Not only that, but Sugar Smacks's tail was moving all about, doing that awful swirling and swishing thing it always did whenever she was around Obi.

"Hey, Obi," she said, "let's play our game! C'mon, touch my paw!" The cat held out her paw for Obi to touch.

"If you don't mind, Sugar Smacks, could you please just pounce on me and get it over with?" asked Obi. "Put me out of my misery."

"Sure, I'd be happy to," replied Sugar Smacks. "But first let's play our game!"

At that moment, Obi heard another cat hop up onto the kitchen table. It was Honey Buns.

"Well, for heaven's sake!" said Honey Buns, staring at Obi in amazement. "That crazy old parrot was right! You are loose!" She focused her eyes on Sugar Smacks and said, "Hey, what's the game you just mentioned? I want to play, too! Can I? Can I?"

Sugar Smacks pulled her paw away from Obi. "Game?" she said, frowning, pretending she had no idea what Honey Buns was talking about. "What game? Nobody is playing a game."

"I heard you say 'game,'" said Honey Buns.

Sugar Smacks chuckled. "You thought I said 'game'? I said 'shame.' You know, as in 'Isn't it a *shame*!'"

"It didn't sound like 'shame,'" said Honey Buns. "It sounded like 'game.'"

"Oh, it was 'shame,' all right," said Sugar Smacks.

"C'mon, Sugar Smacks, let me play, too," said Honey Buns.

"Play what?" asked Sugar Smacks, still playing dumb.

Honey Buns pouted. "Oh, all right, be that way," she said. "But Obi is mine now. So if you'll kindly excuse us."

"Uh, *excuse* me!" said Sugar Smacks. "But *I* was here first. You know what they say: first come, first served."

"Who says *that*?" said Honey Buns. "I don't say that." She peered at Obi and said, "Do you say that, Obi?"

Obi shook her head and said, "No." Which was the truth. She had never said it. She had never had any reason to.

"Well, I say it!" said Sugar Smacks.

"Well, it's two against one," said Honey Buns.

"Where do you get two from?" demanded Sugar Smacks.

"Obi and me."

"Obi doesn't count!" said Sugar Smacks.

"Why not?" asked Honey Buns.

"Because she doesn't! She's a gerbil!"

"So?"

"*So!* Gerbils don't count!"

"Of course they do!" insisted Honey Buns. She glanced at Obi again and said, "You count, don't you, Obi?"

Obi shrugged. "Sure. I guess I do."

"Hey, you keep out of this!" said Sugar Smacks irritably, glowering at Obi. The cat angrily smacked Obi with the furry back of her paw. This, in turn, sent Obi flying off the edge of the kitchen table and into the air. With a soft thud, the little gerbil plopped down on her bum-bum on the tiled floor. She landed in front of the refrigerator. Obi picked herself up—just as Sweetie Smoochkins came strolling into the kitchen from the dining room. The cat stopped and, looking startled as anything, stared at Obi.

"Hey, you are loose!" she exclaimed.

Now, being slapped by Sugar Smacks had two effects on Obi: (1) It allowed her to escape from Sugar Smacks and Honey Buns; and (2) it served as a wake-up call for the little gerbil. Obi realized that, as glum and dispirited as she felt, she wasn't quite ready to let herself be devoured by a cat. Sweetie Smoochkins stepped toward Obi. Her tail began to swirl and dip. Obi, whipping around, bolted for the hallway. She'd only taken a few steps, however, when Sugar Smacks and Honey Buns both sprang down from the kitchen table. The two cats landed in front of Obi, blocking that exit out of the kitchen.

Terrified, Obi froze.

"Looks like we've got you cornered, Fuzzball," said Sweetie Smoochkins, grinning. She was standing near the doorway to the dining room so that eliminated that way out of the kitchen.

Obi's heartbeat quickened as she glanced frantically about the kitchen for another escape route. She spied a narrow, vertical opening—a sort of crevice—between the refrigerator and the cabinet that was beside it. The opening was just wide enough for Obi to slip into, but not the cats. Quickly, Obi turned and darted into the opening.

The cats were caught by surprise. They whirled about and rushed to the refrigerator. The three of them crowded in front of the narrow opening.

"There's no way out, Obi, so you might as well come out," said Sugar Smacks.

"Yeah, if you know what's good for you," said Honey Buns.

Sweetie Smoochkins added, "You'll have to come out sooner or later, Fuzzball. Might as well be sooner than later."

Obi, her heart pounding furiously, did not know what to do. As long as she stayed in the crevice she was safe. But how long could she hide in here?

Honey Buns squished her face against the narrow opening and stuck her paw into the crevice to try and swat Obi. The little gerbil took a step back to avoid the cat's lunging paw. As she did, she stepped on something. Obi looked down. It was a piece of pink notebook paper. It was lying on the filthy crevice floor, right next to a dust-covered Cheerio that had rolled into the crevice long ago. Glancing about, Obi saw that quite a number of small items had fallen into the crevice: a toy jack, a penny, a small rubber ball, and a refrigerator magnet that looked like a hamburger. As she was gazing about at all these things, Obi noticed something about the piece of paper that she was standing upon. Something really astonishing. Rachel's handwriting was on it! Even more startling, Obi's name was written on the paper! Obi, frowning, stepped to the side, bent down, and picked up the piece of paper. She held it up to the light—what little light that fell into the crevice, thanks to Honey Buns's big, fat head blocking the opening. Fortunately, Obi had just enough light to read the note.

Tad—Please feed Obi!!!!!! His food is in the pantry. He gets fed twice a day. And don't forget to fill his water bottle. Thanks!

Rachel

P.S. He loves the yogurt puffballs!!!!!!!!

It was as if a locked door in Obi's troubled heart had suddenly exploded open, letting in a burst of light—beautiful, warm, radiant light. The little gerbil felt so wonderful! So relieved!

And so *loved*!

Rachel had not forgotten Obi! No, not at all! Her adopted mother did love her! And this note proved it!

The note answered so many questions and instantly lifted Obi's spirits. But now she had another question. How on earth had the note ever found its way into this dark, narrow, filthy crevice?

And then, just like that, the mystery got solved. On the opposite side of the kitchen, there was an unexpected sound—that of a key turning in the lock.

Tad was here!

Honey Buns pulled her face from the crevice opening and peered at the kitchen door. Now that Honey Buns's big head wasn't in the way, Obi could see the other two cats. All three of them were gazing at the door. They glanced back at the crevice, then, over at the door again. Clearly, they were having trouble deciding whether to continue to guard Obi or dash to the door and greet Tad when he entered the house. The doorknob jiggled. With loud meows, Honey Buns, Sugar Smacks, and Sweetie Smoochkins raced toward the door.

Obi heard the kitchen door push open. She felt a breeze from outside the house enter the dark crevice.

And then the most astonishing thing happened. From her hiding spot, Obi watched as the sheet of paper with Tad's instructions blew off the kitchen table. Powered by the breeze, it gently floated through the air and landed on the kitchen floor, directly in front of the crevice opening. If the paper had been a little smaller—say, about the size of Rachel's note—it would have floated right into the crevice.

chapter Twenty-five Batteries

Obi quickly figured out what must have happened. Rachel had not forgotten Obi. No, not at all. What she *had* forgotten to do was to put a weight—say, for instance, a salt or pepper shaker—on her note to Tad when she left it on the kitchen table. Evidently, a few hours later, when the boy opened the door to feed the pets, a breeze from outside had blown Rachel's note off the table and into this dark crevice.

Obi remembered the day that the Armstrongs had left for vacation. How could she forget it? It was such a traumatic day! She remembered how windy it had been. She also remembered how all the Armstrongs had been strapped in their human mobile, and how Mr. Armstrong had been backing the human mobile out of the driveway when Rachel, in the backseat, had leaned forward and told her father something that made him stop the vehicle (as well as frown in exasperation).

Rachel and her mother had then come back into the house. But Rachel did not come upstairs. When, later, Obi asked Sugar Smacks what Rachel had done when she was in the house, the cat said that Rachel had written something on a piece of paper. Obviously, she had written this note to Tad telling him to feed Obi. Now Rachel was off on vacation, thinking Obi was happily being fed.

It was a huge relief for Obi to know that her adopted mother had not forgotten her, that she really did love her, after all. How could Obi have thought otherwise? Well, at least she didn't have to worry about *that* anymore!

But there was something Obi still did have to worry about: getting out of this dark, narrow crevice, not to mention getting fed. Being ever so quiet, Obi crept toward the crevice opening and peered out into the kitchen. The cats were hovering about Tad's legs as he poured dry cat food from a small bag into each of their small bowls. As Obi watched, she realized there was something different about Tad. She couldn't quite put her paw on what it was, though. He was wearing a bandanna on his head just as he always did. And he had on his baggy shorts, grubby sandals, and an oversize T-shirt. And goodness knows, his hair was as frizzy and wild as ever. And, of course, he was wearing his earpho—

Wait! That was it! That was what was different about Tad. His earphones! Tad usually had little white earphones plugged into his ears. Today, though, he was listening to music through different earphones. These earphones were saucer-shaped and larger—much larger. Indeed, they covered his entire ears. What's more, the wire that was attached to the earphones led to a round, flat, electronic gizmo that Tad had set on the counter. It was a CD-player, like what Rachel listened to.

"One love, one life," Tad was singing to himself while he listened to his music through the earphones. Having fed the cats, he now stood at the counter, opening a can of dog food with the electric can opener. Tad had a loud, rather nasal, out-of-tune voice—not all that unlike the sound of the electric can opener.

"You got to get it together," sang Tad.

Obi was so glad to see Tad. It meant her long ordeal was finally over. All she had to do was let Tad see her and he would realize that he needed to feed her, too. Obi stepped out into the kitchen. She glanced over at the cats. They were eating from their bowls, with their backs to Obi. Obi began trotting toward Tad. She was halfway across the kitchen floor when she suddenly thought of something. She froze.

Oh, my gosh! What am I doing? she nearly blurted out loud. I can't let Tad see me! He doesn't know anything about me. If he sees me, he won't know who I am. He might think I'm a mouse or, worse, a rat! He might even try to kill me!

Alarmed, Obi turned and raced back into the crevice. Standing just out of sight, she continued to watch Tad as she tried to figure out what she should do.

Over by the counter, Tad dumped the can of dog food into a large bowl. As he set the can down on the counter, he abruptly stopped singing. He picked up the CD-player and examined it.

"What the?" he said with a frown, staring at the CD-player. He shook the CD-player. "Oh, c'mon!" he said in an annoyed voice. "Man, I just put in new batteries!"

Tad stepped over to the drawer where the Armstrongs kept their spoons, forks, and knives. He pulled open the drawer and took out a knife. First, he used the knife to unscrew the little plastic cover on the back of the CD-player. Then he used the knife to pry open the cover. He must have applied too much pressure, because all of a sudden the small batteries that were in the CD-player bounced up into the air. Tad did a little juggling act, trying to catch them all. He was unable to catch even one, though. The batteries went sliding across the floor, rolling every which way. One even rolled into the dark crevice where Obi was hiding.

"Oh, for crying out loud!" exclaimed Tad. He got down on his hands and knees and began picking up the batteries. He crawled over to the refrigerator and peered into the dark crevice. Obi leaped back into the darkness so she couldn't be seen. Tad stuck his hand into the crevice, feeling around for the battery. Obi's heart fluttered at the sight of this human boy's big hand reaching into her hiding place. She inched forward and kicked the battery toward Tad's fingers. His fingers felt the battery and grabbed it.

Whew! That was a close one! thought Obi. But as Tad got to his feet, Obi realized she had made a mistake. A huge mistake! Instead of kicking the battery at Tad, she should have kicked Rachel's note to him! Then he would have pulled the note out, read it, and found out that he needed to feed her!

"Gosh-darn it all!" murmured Obi. She wanted to kick herself, she was so mad.

Out in the kitchen, Tad was now going from kitchen drawer to kitchen drawer, pulling each one open. Evidently, he was looking for new batteries to put in his CD-player.

Tad walked over to the door that led down to the basement. He opened the door, flicked on the overhead light, and disappeared down the stairs. He must be going down to Mr. Armstrong's tool room to look for batteries, thought Obi.

From her hiding spot, Obi could see the CD-player that Tad had left on the kitchen table. She glanced over at the cats. They were still at their bowls, eating. An idea formed in Obi's head. She didn't have much time, but she thought that if she was quick about it, and sneakily quiet, she just might be able to pull it off.

Obi folded Rachel's note in half with her front paws and put it in her mouth. Being very quiet, she crept out of her hiding spot. The cats were hunched over their bowls, with their backs to Obi. Keeping her eyes on them, Obi stole across the floor toward the round kitchen table. She felt like a Jedi knight sneaking past a bunch of thieving aliens. Only instead of a light saber in her mouth, Obi held a note, Rachel's note.

When Obi got to the kitchen table, she silently climbed up the leg of one of the kitchen-table chairs. When she reached the cane seat of the chair, she grabbed the linen tablecloth that hung down from the table, dug her claws in, and pulled herself up onto the tabletop.

Tad's CD-player was lying, faceup, near Rachel's stack of CDs. Obi's plan was to leave the note on top of the CD-player so that Tad would discover it when he came back into the kitchen. Obi's heart thumped wildly as she stepped close to the CD-player. She placed her paw on it to set the note down.

A very unexpected and scary thing happened then. Obi stepped on one of the buttons on the CD-player, and the round lid that covered the CD abruptly flipped open, revealing the CD inside. It startled Obi so much that she gasped and leaped back. She shot a quick glance at the cats. They were still at their bowls, munching happily away. Luckily, they had not heard anything.

Obi was about to push the lid to the CD-player back down when she had the most brilliant idea. If she were to remove the CD that Tad had been listening to and replace it with Rachel's note, there would be no way Tad would miss finding the note. There'd be no chance, for instance, that a breeze might blow it off the table again and onto the floor where Tad would miss seeing it for a second time.

With Rachel's note still in her mouth, Obi took the disc out of the CD-player. This wasn't quite as easy as she'd thought it would be. As Obi quickly discovered, a gerbil's paws are not exactly made for handling CDs. Holding the disc in her front paws, Obi placed it down on the table. Then she dropped Rachel's note into the round, hollow opening of the CD player where Tad's CD had been. She shut the lid on top of Rachel's note.

Perfect! thought Obi.

As Obi turned to leave, her gaze fell upon Tad's CD. It was lying on the table, uncased and unprotected. If Tad was anything like Craig (and as far as Obi could tell, he was a lot like Craig), Tad would not be very happy about seeing his CD exposed like this. Obi remembered one time when Rachel had forgotten to put one of Craig's CDs back into its case. Craig had gone ballistic, yelling and screaming at Rachel and telling her that if his CD got scratched, she was in big, big trouble. The last thing Obi wanted was to annoy Tad. She needed his help too badly. She needed him to feed her!

Obi hurried over and picked up the CD. Now that she had it in her paws, though, what was she to do with it? She glanced around. The only other CDs on the table were the ones that belonged to Rachel.

While Obi stood there, puzzling over what to do, she caught sight of a gray, furry thing just outside the kitchen window.

Oh, no! It was that daffy squirrel again! He was perched in the branches of a young dogwood tree that grew out in the backyard. The squirrel was gaping in at Obi, his jaw hanging open and the most incredulous look on his face. You didn't need to be an expert on squirrels to figure out what was going on inside that scrambled brain. The squirrel obviously thought Obi was stealing Tad's CD.

Obi shook her head to let the squirrel know it wasn't what it looked like. Just then, though, Obi heard human footsteps clomping up the basement stairs.

Tad was on his way back up to the kitchen!

In a panic, Obi stepped over to Rachel's stack of music CDs. By this point, Obi was such a bundle of nerves, she was no longer thinking clearly. She just wanted to get rid of Tad's CD and get off the kitchen table as quickly as possible. She popped open the square, plastic case. Obi gasped in surprise. There was a CD already in the case! Which made sense, of course, when you thought about it—but who had time to think about it? Not Obi! Obi yanked Rachel's CD out of its case and replaced it with Tad's CD. As she closed the top of the case, she could hear Tad's footsteps on the stairs growing louder and louder.

Obi stared at the disc that she was holding in her paws. What was she to do with *this* CD?

By now, Tad's footsteps were almost to the top of the

basement stairs. Obi had run out of time. She had no choice but to drop Rachel's CD right there on the table and flee. With her heart beating fast, Obi darted across the table and leaped.

Sweetie Smoochkins, being closest, heard Obi land on the floor. The cat lifted her head from her bowl and peered curiously over at Obi. It took her a moment to realize whom she was staring at. Her eyes widened with rage.

"Hey, it's Fuzzball! Meeeowww!" cried Sweetie Smoochkins as she whipped around and sprang toward Obi.

Terrified, Obi scrambled to her feet and dove into the crevice between the refrigerator and cabinet. She made it just in the nick of time. Another second and Obi would have been a very tasty after-breakfast treat for Sweetie Smoochkins.

Gasping for breath, Obi picked herself up and raced to the back of the dark crevice. Sweetie Smoochkins sprinted over and thrust her paw in at Obi. But Obi was too far into the crevice for the cat's paw to reach her. Shaken up by what had just happened, Obi was trembling, and her legs felt all wobbly. She glanced around the crevice for something to sit on. She saw the small rubber ball and plopped herself down on it.

Sweetie Smoochkins tried again and again to strike Obi with her paw. Then Honey Buns gave it a shot. Then Sugar Smacks tried. Then Sweetie Smoochkins gave it another valiant effort. Obi, meanwhile, sat on the small red ball and tried to see what Tad was doing. Since the cats were blocking her view, Obi had to really strain her neck to see the boy. Having returned from the basement, Tad now stood by the kitchen table, putting new batteries into the CD-player. He had not yet discovered

Rachel's note. Using the knife, Tad screwed the lid to the battery compartment back onto the CD-player. He slipped his earphones back on over his ears and pushed the Play button on the CD-player.

Obi held her breath.

"*Now* what's the problem?" Tad groaned, frowning in exasperation at the CD-player. He looked as if he was about to fling the CD-player across the room.

Tad pushed the button that flipped open the top of the CD-player. He stared in amazement at the folded pink note that was stuck there.

"Huh?!" he blurted out. "How did *this* get here?"

Tad removed the note. Obi's heart thumped wildly with excitement. At long last, Tad was going to find out about her.

But Tad did not unfold the note. Instead, the boy picked up the CD that lay on the kitchen table. It was Rachel's CD, the one Obi had dropped on the table when she fled. Without even looking at the disc, Tad inserted it into the CD-player. Evidently, he thought it was *his* CD, the one he had been listening to. He pushed the Play button again. While he waited for his music to start playing, Tad picked up Rachel's note and began to unfold it.

The loud, anguished, tortured cry that followed was like no other sound Obi had ever heard before.

"ARRRRGGGGHHHHHHHHH!" Tad roared, yanking the earphones from his ears and dropping the note. "I *hate* this music!"

Tad's scream startled the cats. They leaped high into the air. With frightened meows, they dashed out of the kitchen. Mack let out a bark.

"My poor ears!" wailed Tad as he took the disc out of his CD-player. He peered at the label. "This isn't my CD!" he cried. "What's going on?"

Tad picked up the CD case that was on top of Rachel's stack of CDs. He popped it open.

"Here's *my* CD!" he said. "This is *so* weird!"

He inserted his CD into the CD-player and pushed the Play button again.

"Ah, that's better," he sighed with relief.

While Tad might have been relieved, Obi sure was not. She was devastated. When Tad screamed, he had dropped Rachel's note onto the floor. Obi had come so close to having Tad read the note, only to be foiled again. Disheartened, she plopped down on the small rubber ball and buried her face in her paws.

But then she heard Tad say, "Now, where did that piece of paper go?"

Obi stood up. In the kitchen, she saw Tad bend over, searching the floor for Rachel's note.

"Oh, here it is!" he said, picking up the small piece of pink paper. It had fallen under the kitchen table. He stood and opened the note and read it to himself.

"Oh, my God!" he gasped. "That poor little critter! All this time with no food! I need to feed Obi right this second!"

Obi, hearing this, nearly let out a whoop of joy. She was so thrilled, so elated. Her plan had worked! Tad now knew about her! Knew about her and was going to feed her!

Tad disappeared into the kitchen pantry. He reappeared a moment later, carrying a small plastic bag. And not just any bag. It was the bag of gerbil food! Better still, in his hand Tad held a box of yummy-yum yogurt puffballs!

Obi watched in delight as Tad headed for the hallway to go upstairs to Rachel's bedroom. When the boy walked past the crevice, Obi wanted to cheer. But then Obi thought of something.

Something dreadful.

Oh, my gosh! If Tad finds I'm not in my cage, he's likely to think I've perished from hunger! If he thinks I've perished, he won't have any reason to feed me!

chapter Twenty-eight

Obi-Wan Kenobi Would Have Been Proud

Obi didn't know what to do. Well, that's not quite true. She knew what to do, she just didn't know *how* to do it. She had to get back into her cage before Tad arrived in Rachel's bedroom to feed her. But how was she going to do *that*? Sugar Smacks and Sweetie Smoochkins, having recovered from the shock of hearing Tad scream, had returned to the kitchen. They were now hovering just outside Obi's hiding place, with fierce, determined looks on their faces, waiting for Obi to step out into the kitchen.

As Obi frantically tried to think of a way to get past the cats, her eye fell upon the toy jack that lay on the dusty crevice floor. The metal jack had four spiky prongs and looked more like a weapon than a toy. This gave Obi an idea. She picked up the jack and focused her eyes on Sweetie Smoochkins. The cat was peering into the crevice, trying to see what Obi was doing. Using her front paws, Obi lifted the jack above her head. She was all set to hurl it into Sweetie Smoochkins's face when another thought occurred to her.

If I throw this jack at Sweetie Smoochkins, it's going to really hurt. It might even poke out her eye! It's also going to get Sweetie Smoochkins really mad. She'll be more determined than ever to catch me and tear me limb from limb, and then I'll never get back to my cage!

With a heavy sigh, Obi set the jack down on the floor beside the rubber ball. Obi stared at the ball, remembering something. Once, while in her Gerbil Mobile, she had seen Betsy and Susie—the human twins Betsy and Susie, that is, not the goldfish—playing with the cats in the TV room. The girls kept tossing a small rubber mouse across the room. Every time one of them flung the rubber mouse, the cats chased after it. (Which caused the two girls to shriek with delight.) Could such a thing work with a small rubber ball?

There was only one way to find out.

Obi picked up the rubber ball and took a step back so she was all but invisible in the shadows. She didn't want Sweetie Smoochkins to see what she was about to do.

"Okay, I'm coming out!" shouted Obi. "Ready or not, here I come!"

Obi drew back her paw and flung the ball with all her might. She tossed the ball in such a way that it arched high into the air, right over the heads of Sweetie-Smoochkins and Sugar Smacks.

It worked! Both cats fell for the trick! Sweetie Smoochkins reared up on her hind legs and tried to swat the ball with her front paws before it bounced across the kitchen floor. Sweetie Smoochkins and Sugar Smacks took off after it.

With no cat guarding the entrance of the crevice, Obi dashed out. She made a beeline for the hallway. She was nearly there when Honey Buns appeared in the doorway. Obi froze in her tracks.

"Going somewhere?" asked Honey Buns with an amused grin.

"I need to get back to my cage!" said Obi.

"I don't think so," said Honey Buns.

"Oh, I think so!" replied Obi.

The little gerbil had never spoken in such a brave, bold, defiant manner to one of the cats before. Never! Blinking, Honey Buns stared at Obi with wide, astonished eyes. To be honest, Obi was just as astounded as the cat to hear herself speak this way.

"I don't think so," Honey Buns said again, as if she thought she had been hearing things.

"I think so!" repeated Obi, just as defiantly as before.

And then Obi did something even more shocking. She bent her knees and leaped up into the air, high above Honey Buns's head. While in the air, Obi did not one, not two, but three spectacular somersaults. She landed on the hallway carpet, on the other side of Honey Buns. It was a move right out of a *Star Wars* movie. Obi-Wan Kenobi, that fearless, clever, resourceful Jedi knight, would have been so proud of Obi. Obi, the Jedi gerbil! Oh, if only Obi had been armed with a light saber, she could have lopped off Honey Buns's head while she was in midair. Not that Obi would have done such a thing. She wasn't that kind of gerbil.

You never saw a more astounded and dumbfounded-looking cat. Honey Buns just stood in the doorway, looking absolutely flabbergasted at Obi. As much as Obi would have liked to stay and savor the moment, she had a cage to get back to. She took off, scurrying down the hallway toward the stairs that led up to the second floor. Obi was all set to start hopping up the steps when, upon reaching the foot of the stairs, she glanced upward and halted. Tad was nearly at the top step. Even if Obi hopped up the steps two at a time, there was no way she would be able to catch the boy, let alone pass him. Behind her, Obi heard galloping footsteps. She glanced back and saw Sweetie Smoochkins, Honey Buns, and Sugar Smacks sprinting toward her, their eyes gleaming with fury. Obi quickly glanced about, trying to figure out what to do. Suddenly, it dawned on her that she was standing right in front of the old grandfather clock—where Mr. Durkins had told her there was an entrance to the secret passageway. But even if Obi were to escape into the secret passageway, she still would never be able to get back to her cage before Tad.

Unless, of course, she created a diversion.

The diversion, Obi realized, would have to be good and loud. *Really* good and loud. Otherwise Tad, with those darn earphones over his ears, would never hear it.

Obi spun about and faced the cats. She threw her front paws up into the air the way she had once seen a human bank robber on TV do after he'd been nabbed red-handed by the police. Obi even cried out, "I give up!"

The cats dashed up to Obi and stopped. They quickly formed a circle around her. "Well, it's about time you came to your senses," said Sweetie Smoochkins.

"You better not try any more tricks!" growled Honey Buns.

"So who gets me?" asked Obi, glancing from one cat to the other.

"What do you mean, who gets you?" asked Sugar Smacks.

"Well, there are three of you and just one of me," replied Obi. "I'm not very big. Plus, don't forget, I haven't eaten a decent meal in days. I'm not the plump, tender little gerbil I once was. Even so, I bet I'm still a pretty scrumptious meal. You're not really going to *share* me, are you?"

Sweetie Smoochkins flicked her eyes first at Honey Buns, then at Sugar Smacks. "Fuzzball has a point," she said.

"Well, I just assumed that I'd get Obi," said Honey Buns.

"Well, you assumed wrong!" said Sweetie Smoochkins.

"Hey, I'm the only one who ever plays with the gerbil!" said Sugar Smacks. "She's mine!"

"No, mine!" declared Honey Buns, and hissed at Sugar Smacks.

Sugar Smacks hissed right back at Honey Buns. Sweetie Smoochkins, meanwhile, made a move toward Obi. Honey Buns, seeing this, hissed and stepped in front of the other cat. Sweetie Smoochkins hissed right back and took a swipe at Honey Buns's face with her paw. Just as Obi had hoped, a fight broke out. A huge, ugly, *loud* fight, with lots of hissing.

Obi glanced up the stairs. Tad had reached the top step. He was just about to disappear down the upstairs hallway when, even with earphones covering his ears, he heard the cats hissing and fighting.

"Hey, what's going on down there?" cried Tad, frowning, as he gazed quizzically down the staircase.

The cats kept right on fighting. With the bag of gerbil food in one hand and the box of yogurt puffballs in the other, Tad came hurrying down the stairs.

"Hey! Hey! Hey!" he cried. "No fighting! Stop it this instant, you cats!"

Obi waited for just the right moment. Then, when no one was paying any attention to her, she quietly slipped under the old grandfather clock and squeezed into the hole that led into the secret passageway.

"Hey, where did Fuzzball go?" she heard Sweetie Smoochkins blurt out.

"She was just here a second ago!" said Sugar Smacks.

"She couldn't have just vanished!" said Honey Buns.

"This is all your fault!" declared Sweetie Smoochkins.

"*My* fault?" cried Honey Buns.

And with that, the fight erupted again.

"Hey, you cats! Stop it!" bellowed Tad.

Obi chuckled to herself as she made her way through the darkened passageway. Obi, Jedi gerbil, strikes again! Her eyes were just beginning to adjust to the dim light when, up ahead, she spied a mysterious small smudge. Obi couldn't make out what it was. Whatever it was, it was right in the middle of the secret passageway. As Obi got closer, she saw that the smudge was a mouse—an old, hunched-over mouse. Why, it was old Mr. Durkins! He stood in the passageway, blocking Obi's path. In his paws, he held a plastic fork that was missing two of its prongs.

"Get out of my way, Mr. Durkins," said Obi.

The old mouse shook his head. "I've got to save you, kid! I can't let you go back to them!"

"I said get out of my way!"

"You're making a mistake, kid!"

"I don't want to hurt you, Mr. Durkins! Now, please, get out of my way!"

But the old mouse did not budge.

"You're a rodent, not a human!" he cried. "You don't belong with them!"

Obi squatted and got ready to charge. The old mouse saw this and braced himself for Obi's attack. He bent his legs and aimed the prongs of his plastic fork toward Obi like it was a spear.

Head lowered, Obi rushed forward. She plowed into Mr. Durkins, easily tossing him aside. As the old mouse fell down onto the dusty floorboard, Obi heard a loud, horrible crack.

The sound terrified Obi. Oh, no, she had broken poor old Mr. Durkins's back!

As it turned out, it wasn't poor old Mr. Durkins's back that had snapped in two. It was the plastic fork. Mr. Durkins sat on the floor, holding his broken plastic fork, looking dazed and gasping for breath.

Obi felt terrible that she had knocked over an old, crippled mouse. She leaned down and helped Mr. Durkins back up onto his feet.

"Sorry, Mr. Durkins, but you wouldn't let me pass."

"Don't go, Obi!" cried the old mouse, sounding desperate, as Obi turned to leave. "You're making a mistake! A big mistake! She doesn't love you!"

Obi stopped and swung around. She was fuming

mad. "Yes, I made a big mistake," she said. "My mistake was that I let myself believe that Rachel didn't love me. But she does love me! And I think you know that, Mr. Durkins. You spy on us all the time. You see how she treats me and you can't stand it. You're just a miserable old mouse with a shriveled-up heart who doesn't know how to love! You just know how to hate! Well, I'm sorry, Mr. Durkins, but I don't hate Rachel—or any of the Armstrongs! And I'm not going to end up like *you*!"

Before Mr. Durkins could say a word, Obi turned and continued down the dark passageway. She had to really hustle now. Mr. Durkins had caused her to lose valuable time. By this point, Tad had surely settled the cats' fight and was on his way up the stairs to Rachel's bedroom. Anxious to get back to her cage before Tad, Obi broke into a run. But it was very dark inside the secret passageway, and Obi was not at all familiar with where she was going. It seemed like she should have come to the hole that led into Rachel's bedroom. But she didn't see any little opening with light peeping from it. Where was it? Obi ran faster. Finally, she spotted the exit. Quickly, Obi squeezed herself through. As she stepped out of the secret passageway, Obi stopped and stared. This wasn't Rachel's bedroom! She had overshot her mark—she was in Craig's dimly lit bedroom. There was no time to go back into the secret passageway and retrace her steps. Obi would just have to pass through Craig's bedroom to get back to her cage.

Boa, the corn snake, was the first to spot Obi. He was in his aquarium on Craig's desk. As Obi dashed across the carpet, the snake called out in his deep, melodious, singsongy voice, "Bohh-waa! Oohh-bee! Bohh-waa! Oohh-bee! Bohh-waaa! Oohh-beeee!"

José, the tarantula, whose aquarium sat beside Boa's, was in a tizzy. He sprang about on the sand that covered the bottom of his aquarium and cried, "Señorita Obi! There she goes! There she goes! Don't just lie there, Boa! Go get her!"

Obi heard a loud *thunk!* as the snake's reptilian head banged against the glass aquarium.

"The screen, you dimwit, the screen! Not the glass!" shouted José, groaning in exasperation. "You were supposed to go through the screen on top of your cage! Unbelievable! The incompetence I've got to deal with!"

"Hey, Oohh-bee!" called Boa. "What's the big rush?"

Without slowing down, Obi waved a paw at Boa and José and called out, "Sorry, guys! Gotta run!"

"Oh, don't go!" Boa called out. "Stay! We're your pals,

Bo-wa and José—you know, the boa constrictor and the spider."

"Spider?!" roared José indignantly, hopping up and down. "I'm not a spider! Can't you get that through your thick skull? I'm a tarantula! A ta-rant-u-*laaaa!*"

Craig's bedroom door was shut. Obi dropped down to her stomach and squeezed under the door. Then she sprang up and ran down the upstairs hallway toward Rachel's bedroom. She was nearly there when, farther down the hallway, Tad appeared, coming up the stairs. He was carrying Obi's bag of gerbil food, the box of yogurt puffballs, and—incredibly—the three cats! Apparently, Tad's way of brokering peace with the cats was to cuddle them in his arms.

Obi rolled her eyes and dashed into Rachel's bedroom.

Obi ran to Rachel's dresser, scrambled up the lamp cord, hopped across the top of the dresser, pulled open her cage door, leaped into her cage, then, snapped the cage door shut with the end of her tail—just as Tad walked into Rachel's bedroom. Exhausted, her heart hammering, Obi flopped down onto the mound of cedar shavings that she had built to fool the cats into thinking she was underneath it, sleeping. Tad, still cradling the cats in his arms, walked quickly over to the dresser and gazed into Obi's cage.

"Thank God! You're still alive!" he cried, sounding truly glad and relieved.

The cats, on the other hand, did not look glad. Not one bit! They scowled and hissed at Obi. Honey Buns even swiped her paw in Obi's direction.

Tad stared at the cats. He looked shocked, even disgusted. "What *is* your problem?" he asked them. "This poor little critter hasn't had any food or water for the past week, and *this* is how you act? Just for that, from here on out, I'm feeding Obi before I feed any of *you*! Now get out of here!" Tad dropped the cats ignominiously onto the floor.

The cats, being cats, landed on their feet. They stared in astonishment at Tad. Clearly, they could not believe this was really happening to them.

"Go on, you heard what I said!" cried Tad, glaring at the cats. "Beat it!" He stamped his foot to show he meant business.

The cats, frightened, took off, scampering out of Rachel's bedroom.

Tad turned and peered kindly down at Obi. From the box of yogurt puffballs, he withdrew a puffball, a red one. He opened Obi's cage door and held the puffball on the palm of his big hand. "Here you go, little fella," he said tenderly.

Obi got up and shyly stepped over to Tad's palm and nibbled on the puffball. It felt so weird to eat out of a teenage boy's hand. But, wow, did that yogurt puffball taste scrumptious!

"It was the strangest thing, Obi," said Tad, talking to Obi as if she was a human. "I found a note that Rachel had written. It was in my CD-player. I have no idea how it got there. It was like, you know, a miracle!"

Obi, chewing, gazed up at Tad with the most innocent-looking expression on her face. It was as if her face said, "Gee, I wonder how *that* could've happened?"

Tad was true to his word. From that day onward, whether it was morning or evening, he fed Obi before he fed the cats or, for that matter, any of the other pets in the Armstrong household. Obi did not leave her cage after that morning. She had no reason to. Thanks to Tad, she now had plenty of food and water. In fact, Tad had a tendency to *over*feed the little gerbil. But that was okay: too much food was better than no food at all. Besides, Obi just ate what she needed, never stuffing herself.

In the days that followed, Obi went back to her old routine. She ran on her exercise wheel. She went back to taking her late-morning naps. (Fortunately, she no longer had anymore nightmares.) She even took time out of her day to watch the squirrel, that wacko trapeze artist, zip back and forth across the telephone and electrical wires. One time the squirrel happened to glance over at Rachel's bedroom window and spotted Obi inside her cage. He scurried up the slanted roof to the window. "I see they've got you locked up again," he said.

Obi decided to have a little fun. She couldn't resist. "Me? Locked up?" she scoffed, with a mischievous look in her eyes. "They haven't built a cage yet that can hold me!" And just to show the squirrel, she pushed open her cage door. Well, *that* did it for the squirrel. His eyes bugged out, his jaw dropped open, and he fled.

Just like old times, Obi still had the occasional feline visitor. Sweetie Smoochkins, Honey Buns, and Sugar Smacks all paid visits. Sweetie Smoochkins demanded to know how on earth Obi, the little fuzzball, had escaped from the cats that morning in the downstairs hallway. It was as if she had simply vanished and then magically reapeared in her cage. Honey Buns vowed to get revenge. Sugar Smacks begged Obi to play their game again. "Oh, come on, don't be a wet blanket!" she said as she wiggled her paw in between the bars of Obi's cage. "Touch my paw!" Obi kindly but firmly refused.

And that was something that was very different about the little gerbil. Before discovering Rachel's note, Obi would never have said no to the cats if they wanted to do something but Obi didn't. She would have been much too frightened. But food wasn't the only thing Obi had gained during the Armstrongs' absence. She had gained confidence in herself. The confidence to be strong and firm and, if need be, to say no.

Late one morning a few days later, Obi was on her exercise wheel, running, when outside the house she heard the *thunk!* of a human mobile door slam shut. Obi thought nothing of it; she was always hearing a human mobile door slam in the neighborhood. But then she heard another door slam outside the house, and she realized that the noise was much closer than she'd at first thought. Indeed, it sounded like it was in the Armstrongs' driveway!

Obi leaped off her exercise wheel and scrambled up the tube to her bedroom tower. What she saw when she peered out the domed plastic skylight filled Obi's heart with tremendous joy.

The Armstrongs were home, back from their vacation. And there, down below, was Rachel, her adopted mother, standing with the rest of her family in the driveway, waiting impatiently for her father to open up the house!

"Come on, Dad, hurry!" Rachel was saying. "I need to see Obe!"

Downstairs, Obi heard a key turn in the kitchen

door. Then she heard Mack bark in the TV room. Then she heard the kitchen door open. Then the cats began to meow. Then she heard her adopted mother's voice cry out, "Hey, Dad, look—my CDs! You left them on the kitchen table!" And then Obi heard the sweetest sound of all: footsteps urgently tearing up the stairs to the bedroom hallway. A moment later, Rachel, tanned and wearing a brand-new T-shirt that said CAPE COD across the front, hurried into the bedroom. She looked absolutely delighted to see Obi.

"Hey, Obe, I'm back!" she cried as she tapped the top of Obi's domed bedroom skylight. "See what I've got for you!" She held up a small white bag.

Obi, thrilled, raced down to her living room. Rachel opened the cage door and reached into Obi's cage. The girl held out her hand, palm up, fingers outstretched, so Obi could step aboard—which Obi was only too happy to do. Rachel brought Obi out of her cage. She set the little gerbil down on the bedroom floor, and then she herself sat down on the carpet.

"Look what I brought back for you," Rachel said. She stuck her hand into the small white bag and pulled out some postcards. "These are all the places we went to on our vacation."

Rachel held up one of the postcards for Obi to see.

It showed a crowded beach by the ocean. Four words arched like a rainbow across a dazzling blue summer sky: *Greetings from Cape Cod*.

The next postcard Rachel held up for Obi to see was from Maine. It showed a photo of a huge red lobster. The third postcard was from New Hampshire. It showed a girl in a two-piece bathing suit waterskiing behind a motorboat on a lake. The last postcard was from Vermont. It showed a bunch of cows standing about in a lush green meadow.

"Thank you so much!" Obi wanted to say to her adopted mother.

"Here's what I thought we could do with them," said Rachel. She sprang to her feet and placed the postcards around Obi's cage like she was planting flowers. She stuck the bottom edges of the postcards in the tight space between the bars at the base of Obi's cage. She inserted each postcard so that the picture side faced into her cage, so Obi would be able to see the photos when she was in her living room.

"Cool, huh? Now you have pictures to look at, you lucky stiff!" said Rachel cheerfully as she plopped back down onto the floor.

But that wasn't what Obi was thinking. She was thinking what a nifty fence the postcards would make.

Now Sugar Smacks, Honey Buns, and Sweetie Smooch-kins would no longer be able to stick their paws in between the bars of Obi's cage.

"Look what else I got for you," said Rachel. From the little white bag, she pulled out a small packaged item. "Cheddar cheese from Vermont!" she cried, unwrapping the paper that was around the small chunk of cheese. "I got it at an old country store. Oh, Obi, I missed you so much!"

"And I missed you so much, too!" Obi wanted so desperately to tell her adopted mother.

"You poor thing," said Rachel. "I bet you've been bored stiff while I've been on vacation, haven't you?"

If you only knew, thought Obi.

Rachel reached over and lovingly stroked Obi on top of her furry head. As the girl did this, Obi had the distinct feeling that the two of them were being secretly watched. Obi couldn't be absolutely sure, of course, but she was nearly certain that a small creature, peeking out through a little hole in the bedroom wall near the clothes closet, was closely observing them.

That night, while the Armstrongs were all in their beds, sound asleep, Obi stole out of her cage. In her mouth, she carried one of the gifts that Rachel had brought back from her vacation for Obi: the chunk of Cheddar cheese. The first thing Obi had done after Rachel returned the gerbil to her cage was to set the cheese aside, near her refrigerator. As tempted as Obi was to gobble it up, she had not touched the cheese. Now, hurrying across the floor of Rachel's darkened bedroom, Obi quietly stepped out into the upstairs hallway. The hallway was lit by the soft glow of a night-light plugged into an electric socket on the wall. The night-light lit the way for Obi as she made her way down the hallway to the steps that led up to the attic door. She began hopping up the stairs. At the top step, Obi crawled underneath the attic door. She trotted across the very dark attic to where the opening of the secret passageway was located behind the pair of ski boots. She set the piece of cheese down on the old floorboards.

"Mr. Durkins," whispered Obi. "Are you here?"

There was no answer. But Obi could have sworn she saw the small silhouette of a mouse disappear behind the dark shape of an old wicker basket.

"I brought you something, Mr. Durkins," said Obi. "Cheddar cheese—your absolute favorite."

Obi waited, but the old mouse did not respond.

"I'll leave it for you," said Obi. "You can eat it whenever you feel like it."

Obi turned and started for the attic door. She had gone only a few steps when, behind her, a voice suddenly spoke, that of an old mouse.

"Thank you, Obi."

Obi swung about. In the bright moonlight that was slipping through the small attic window, she saw the little, hunched-over form of old Mr. Durkins limp out from behind the basket. He looked so sad and alone. It must be hard, Obi thought, to have lost your entire family. Had that not happened, Obi wondered, would Mr. Durkins be a different mouse today, a kinder, less hateful mouse?

As Obi and Mr. Durkins gazed at each other, Obi remembered how the old mouse had fed her one of the cookies that Tad had dropped in the bedroom hallway. This, in turn, made Obi wonder about something else. When the old mouse said he had caused Tad to drop the cookies in the hallway, right in front of Rachel's bedroom doorway, had he done it so the boy might look over and see Obi and realize he needed to feed her? Or had the old mouse done it simply to get himself a cookie? Obi started to open her mouth to ask, but then changed her mind. No, she told herself, it's better I don't find out. If he did do it just to get himself a cookie, it's better not to know. I'd rather think the best of the old mouse and leave it at that, she said to herself. She quietly turned and left.

Back in her cage, Obi made herself comfy up in her bedroom. As she lay nestled in the fresh, fragrant cedar shavings (in addition to everything else, Rachel had cleaned Obi's cage that afternoon), Obi thought about her big secrets, all three of them. Well, true, they weren't really secrets anymore. Mr. Durkins, after all, knew that Obi knew how to read. And the old mouse also knew—as did the cats and the other pets in the Armstrong household, not to mention that nutty squirrel—that Obi could leave her cage at will. And the last secret, the secret passageway, wasn't really Obi's secret anyway; it was old Mr. Durkins's.

Obi suddenly felt herself growing drowsy. She closed her eyes and, as she drifted off to sleep, she thought how lucky she was to be loved, and how nice it was to have three secrets (even though they weren't really secrets), and how handy they would come in for any future adventures.

Little did Obi know that one was about to happen sooner than she would ever dream.